GIFTED
SPEAK
No EVIL

Also available:

Gifted: Out of Sight, Out of Mind

Gifted: Better Late Than Never

Gifted: Here Today, Gone Tomorrow

Gifted: Finders Keepers

Gifted: Now You See Me

GIFTED
SPEAK
NO EVIL

MARILYN KAYE

KINGFISHER
NEW YORK

KINGFISHER
LONDON & NEW YORK

Copyright © Marilyn Kaye 2011
Published in the United States by Kingfisher,
175 Fifth Ave., New York, NY 10010
Kingfisher is an imprint of Macmillan Children's Books, London.
All rights reserved.

Distributed in the U.S. by Macmillan, 175 Fifth Ave., New York, NY 10010
Distributed in Canada by H.B. Fenn and Company Ltd., 34 Nixon Road,
Bolton, Ontario L7E 1W2

Library of Congress Cataloging-in-Publication data has been applied for.

ISBN: 978-0-7534-6564-6

Kingfisher books are available for special promotions and premiums.
For details contact: Special Markets Department,
Macmillan, 175 Fifth Ave., New York, NY 10010.

For more information, please visit www.kingfisherbooks.com

Typeset by Ellipsis Books Limited, Glasgow, U.K.
Printed and bound in the U.K. by CPI Mackays, Chatham ME5 8TD
1 3 5 7 9 8 6 4 2
0211

For Baptiste Latil,
who remembers all my stories

CHAPTER ONE

THE BOY KNOWN AS Carter Street was dreaming.

In his dream, he was in an empty space. There were no windows and no lights, but it wasn't dark, just a dull, bland gray. He was standing because there was nowhere to sit—no chairs, no sofa. He couldn't even sit on the floor because there didn't seem to be a floor. Maybe it wasn't a room at all. He could have been hanging in the air. Or he might have been inside his own head.

But the room, the space, wherever he was—it wasn't completely empty. There was a big television. And an unseen hand turned it on.

What he saw on the screen was vaguely familiar, like a rerun of a show he'd seen before. A young boy, maybe 11 or 12 years old, was riding on a roller coaster. He was accompanied by two shadowy, larger figures sitting on either side of him—the boy's parents? The boy was laughing, throwing his arms up in the air as his car went into a steep descent.

The vision on the screen dissolved and was replaced by another image. The same boy, with the same shadowy figures, at a dining table. Then he saw the boy splashing in a swimming pool. And now the boy was running around a baseball diamond. Then, abruptly, that unseen hand turned off the TV and the screen went dark.

That was when he woke up. For a moment he just lay in the bed very still and stared at the white ceiling above him. That boy in the dream . . . Did he know him? Maybe, maybe not. But there was definitely a connection. Whoever he was, the boy had been turned off, and Carter Street could relate to that.

He sat up and looked around. There was no television in this room, but it wasn't dark and empty. Light streamed in from a window. There was a desk, a chest of drawers, a sink with a mirror over it. There was even a picture on a wall—a small brown puppy lapping water in a bowl. Did the boy in his dream have a dog? No, because his mother was allergic to dog hair.

But he couldn't have known that, could he? Not if he didn't know the boy. Anyway, it was just a dream. He shook his head vigorously as if he could shake out the memory of it, but he knew it would linger. They always did, those dreams.

He didn't want to remember dreams—he had to concentrate on the present. His name, for example. Carter Street. At least, that was what everyone called him. And his location . . . He wasn't in the home of his foster family, the Grangers. And he wasn't in Madame's "gifted" class at Meadowbrook Middle School. Then it came back to him: he was in a place called Harmony House, a special place for teenagers who were in trouble. Was he in trouble? He didn't know and he didn't care. He wasn't in danger, that much he knew for sure, and that was all that mattered. He wasn't cold, and he had a roof over his head and a bed to sleep in. He wasn't hungry—well, maybe he was, just a little, but he knew that he'd be having food very soon. So everything was okay.

He got out of bed, went to the sink, and filled a plastic cup with water from the faucet. He took the cup over to the windowsill, where a plant was sitting. The plant hadn't been there when he arrived. It had been sent by his teacher, Madame, with a note that read, "We miss you."

The words didn't make much sense to him. How could anyone miss him? Even when he was physically in that class, he wasn't really there. He barely existed, no matter where he was. He made no impact on the class, and no one paid any attention to him. They wouldn't notice if he wasn't there.

Another paper had come with the plant—instructions for how to take care of it. He had to keep it warm, and he had to give it water every day. It had no other needs, just shelter and nourishment. Just like Carter Street.

After watering the plant, he continued with the same routine he'd been following since he'd arrived three days earlier. He washed his face, brushed his teeth, and got dressed. Then he left the room, closing the door behind him. He turned to the right and walked to the corner. He was aware of other boys coming out of rooms and moving in the same direction, but he didn't speak to any of them. He couldn't, even if he'd wanted to.

He descended a flight of stairs. At the bottom of the stairs, he went into the room on his left. At the entrance, a smiling man said, "Good morning, Carter." It wasn't a question or a demand, so Carter didn't have to do anything. He walked on to the serving area.

He joined a line of residents to pick up his breakfast tray, and when he received it, he took it to a table and sat down. There were others at the table. On his first day, a couple of them had spoken to him, but now, after three days of no responses, they'd stopped. He didn't particularly want to look at them, but they were in his range of vision, so he couldn't avoid seeing them. A tall boy, light brown hair, glasses. Another boy, darker hair, wearing a green shirt. A girl, blond hair. She had tiny sparkling stones in the lobes of her ears. None of this was important. He just registered the facts. They were talking, but their words meant nothing to him. Not until the boy in the green shirt spoke directly to him.

"Could you pass the salt?"

He understood this as a question that demanded an action. He picked up the salt shaker and handed it to him.

"Thanks," the boy said.

He knew what that meant—the boy was expressing appreciation for Carter's effort. But the word wasn't important, it didn't require a response, and now he could address his food. Food was important. He knew what was in the bowl—cereal, milk, fruit—but that didn't matter. All that mattered was the fact that he could eat it and then he wouldn't be hungry.

When he finished eating, he remained in his seat and watched the big clock on the wall. When it displayed a particular time, he rose, carried his tray to a conveyor belt, and left the dining room. He couldn't go back to his room, though. He had an appointment.

Turning a corner, he went to a door and opened it. A woman at a desk spoke to him. "Hello, Carter. You can go right in. Doctor Paley is waiting for you."

Carter went through the inner door.

"Hello, Carter," the doctor said. "Sit down."

Carter did as he was told and waited while the plump, balding man adjusted the video camera on a table. At the first meeting, the doctor had asked Carter if he would mind if their sessions were recorded, and Carter had offered no objection. Why would he? Being recorded didn't hurt.

"How are you today?" Dr. Paley asked.

Carter was stumped. He couldn't deal with questions like that. After three days of meetings, hadn't the man figured that out? His foster family, Madame, his class-mates—none of them asked him this question anymore because they knew he couldn't answer it. And why should he? Surely the doctor could look at him and see that he wasn't in pain, that he was breathing, that he was physically intact. Nothing about him was any different than it was the day before.

When he didn't respond, Dr. Paley didn't press the question. He just went on speaking.

"I don't know very much about you, Carter. Nobody does. And that's because you don't know much about yourself, do you?"

Carter didn't answer, and Dr. Paley didn't seem to expect him to. He continued talking without a pause.

"The big question, of course, is why? It's possible that you have a condition known as amnesia, an inability to remember. You don't even seem to know your own name." He shuffled through some papers on his desk. "According to your history, you were found here in this city on Carter Street and brought to a hospital. The authorities at the hospital needed a name for you, so this is the name that was decided on."

Carter gazed at him steadily and waited for him to say something Carter didn't already know.

"There's no indication as to how this amnesia

developed," Dr. Paley went on. He picked up another folder and opened it. "The authorities finally sent over your medical records, and I've studied them. Some cases of amnesia occur when the subject receives a severe blow to the head, but the scans you were given show no indication of any trauma. It's possible that you experienced some sort of an infection—a high fever, perhaps, or a virus that affected the part of your brain that stores memory. But blood tests gave no indication of recent illness."

He turned a page and continued. "You were given a battery of tests to determine general intelligence and motor skills. You responded appropriately. Your hearing was tested, and it appears to be normal." He looked up. "But you can't speak. This puzzled the examiners, since they couldn't find anything wrong with your vocal cords or your larynx."

Dr. Paley studied Carter thoughtfully. "But now we know that you *are* physically capable of speaking. A classmate witnessed this. You spoke to a woman . . ." he glanced down at the paper. "Serena Hancock."

The mere sound of the name made Carter want to flinch. Serena . . . yes. She could make him speak. He

8

didn't know how she did it, but he remembered the ease with which the words left his mouth. He wished he couldn't remember what he said.

He hadn't intended to answer her questions, but he didn't seem to have any control when he was with her. And he wasn't capable of lying. So when Serena asked him about his classmates, he told her what he knew, despite the fact that the information was supposed to be kept secret. In class, Madame was always telling them not to reveal anything about their special gifts. Carter didn't have to worry about himself—he had no gift. But they weren't supposed to talk about each other. That's what he'd done, and he knew it was wrong. He had disobeyed.

Dr. Paley closed the folder. "Your teacher has told me that this woman, Serena Hancock, is a member of a group that has a special interest in your gifted classmates. These people have some sort of plan to use the students for criminal purposes. Now, I have a question for you, Carter. Do you *want* to help these people?"

Want . . . It was one of those words that puzzled Carter. He knew what it meant, because he'd wanted things before: food when he was hungry, water when

9

he was thirsty, warmth when he was cold. But the way Dr. Paley had just used the word—he didn't understand.

Dr. Paley sighed. "Let me ask you something else. Do you like your classmates? Or do you *dislike* your classmates?"

Like, dislike . . . Carter just looked at the doctor blankly. What was he talking about? He knew the words, he knew the dictionary definitions, he'd heard people use these words in conversation. But they didn't apply to him.

"Carter, I want to know what you're feeling."

Feeling . . . Carter knew the feeling of hunger, thirst, cold, heat, pain. He wasn't having any of those sensations at that moment.

"Are you sad? Are you angry? Are you sorry?"

Now Carter sort of understood what the doctor was asking, and he knew he couldn't provide an answer. Dr. Paley might just as well have been asking a blind person what he was seeing.

Carter Street didn't have those kinds of feelings.

Chapter Two

I F AMANDA BEESON WAS forced at gunpoint to say something nice about the gifted class, she'd have to admit that it was rarely boring, unlike geography or algebra. This class was unpredictable. Sure, sometimes Madame would go on and on about how they had to control their gifts, how they shouldn't reveal the nature of their gifts, blah, blah, blah, but there was always the chance something could happen during the class. Jenna might reveal something truly bizarre that she'd read in someone's mind. Like the time she told them she'd read the mind of a waiter in a fast-food hamburger place who wanted to pluck a strand of hair from his head and mix it into the ground beef. Or Emily could tell them who would win that season's *American Idol*. Something exciting or even dangerous could happen. Charles might decide to rearrange the desks with his telekinetic powers. Someone might tease Martin and he'd respond by kicking a hole in the wall. In a room full of people with extraordinary talents, there was always the possibility of a surprise or two.

Of course, this didn't mean Amanda *liked* the class. Her main objection to it was the fact that she didn't belong there. She'd known this the first time she was sent into the room, and she became more and more convinced of this every day. Nothing that went on in this class really applied to *her*.

For example, at that very moment, Madame was encouraging them to participate in a discussion that was completely irrelevant to Amanda.

"Class, we've spent a lot of time talking about how you can control your gifts, how you can stop these gifts from emerging and interfering with your own lives. You've practiced techniques involving concentration, meditation, special breathing rhythms. Some of you have made excellent progress. Martin, you've seen changes in your behavior, haven't you?"

Amanda glanced without much interest at the wimpy kid she'd never paid much attention to, and it dawned on her that he was becoming less wimpy. He'd grown over the past few months. His face had lost its babyish look, and he hadn't been whining so much lately. When he spoke, she realized his voice was deeper now, too.

"Well, yeah. My grandfather nags me a lot, and sometimes I can feel a lot of anger building up inside me. I know I could let it out and really hurt him. But I don't."

"That doesn't count," Ken declared. "I mean, he's your grandfather, for crying out loud. You're not going to hit your own grandfather."

"You don't know my grandfather," Martin retorted. "And right this minute, I'm not feeling very kindly toward *you*."

Amanda hid a smile as Ken seemed to flinch slightly. Ken was a former athlete, still in great shape, but he knew as they all did that Martin could send him flying out of the window with a single blow.

"But," Martin added, "the point is, I can control my gift when my grandfather teases me."

"Very good," Madame said with approval. "There's another aspect to your gifts that we need to take into consideration. From our discussions, it seems that most of you—maybe *all* of you—were not born with these gifts. The gifts seem to have emerged as a response to a situation, an experience, or a feeling. Tracey, you understand this, don't you?"

Tracey nodded. "People ignored me, so I felt invisible. And I felt it so strongly that I started to disappear."

"Charles, would you like to comment on how feelings brought about your gift?"

Charles shrugged. "It's not a feeling, it's the situation. I'm in a wheelchair. I can't walk, so I move stuff with my mind."

Madame smiled. "A lot of people are in wheelchairs, Charles, but they don't develop telekinetic powers. Do you remember the first time you were aware of your gift?"

"Yeah, I was in bed, and I wanted this comic book that was on the other side of the room. And I was too lazy to get into my wheelchair, so I made it come to me."

"And how did you feel when you realized what you could do?" Madame asked.

"Good," Charles said promptly.

"Why?" Madame asked.

"Because . . . because I hated not being able to do some stuff for myself. And now I could."

Madame nodded. "You see, Charles, feelings *are* involved. If you'd been content with your situation, you might not have developed the gift."

Ken broke in. "Madame, what's the point?"

Amanda looked at him gratefully. This was exactly what she was wondering, too. Thank goodness for Ken—the one person in the class she could connect with.

Madame raised her eyebrows. "Excuse me, Ken?"

"Okay, I get it, we got our gifts because we had strong feelings about something. I felt guilty about my best friend getting killed when we crashed into each other on the football field, so I started hearing his voice from beyond the grave. And then all these other dead people jumped in and started talking to me. But I don't care how I got the stupid gift. I just want to control it so I don't have to listen to these—these ghosts, or whatever they are."

"But you can't control your gifts unless you understand them," Madame argued. "You have to dig deeper into your feelings if you want to manage these gifts. And you can't all do this in the same way. Not only because each gift is different, but also because each of you is at a unique level in terms of control. Some of you, for example, can summon your gifts at will."

Some students must have looked confused, because she explained.

"What I'm saying is that some of you can call on your gifts when you need them. Like Charles."

Charles beamed. "I can make anything move whenever I want it to move." To illustrate this, he stared at Madame's purse, which hung on the back of her chair. The bag began to rise.

"Charles," Madame warned.

The purse went back to its place.

"Others of you are less capable of bringing your gifts out when you want to. Tracey, you don't have complete control yet, do you?"

"But I'm getting better at it," Tracey said.

Whatever, Amanda thought. This is such a total waste of time.

"Amanda thinks this is a waste of time," Jenna piped up.

Amanda shot her a dirty look. She knew how to block Jenna from reading her mind, but she'd let her guard down.

"Jenna, you know you're not supposed to read your classmates' minds," Madame scolded. "But this is another example of my point. Did Amanda's thought just come to you?"

"No," Jenna replied. "She looked like she wasn't paying much attention, so I was curious to know what she was thinking about."

"In other words," Madame said, "you read her mind intentionally—which, of course, is wrong, because Amanda's thoughts are her own and none of your business. But you did provide an example of what I'm talking about. You have control of your gift. You can decide whether or not to read someone's mind."

Jenna nodded. "Yeah, I can pretty much do it whenever I want. Unless someone knows how to block me. And remembers to do it," she added, with a wicked glance at Amanda. Amanda ignored her.

"I suspect," Madame said, "that all of you are capable of calling upon your gifts when you want them to appear. But some of you haven't yet achieved that level of control."

This is so *not interesting for me*, Amanda thought. She kept the thought in the back of her mind so Jenna couldn't read it, but Madame was getting very good at reading her students' expressions.

"Amanda, do you really think this discussion is a waste of time?"

Amanda now had to admit to herself that there was another decent aspect of the gifted class. You could say what you really thought and not get into trouble.

"For me, it's a waste of time," she declared honestly. "I know how to control my gift. As long as I don't feel sorry for someone, I won't take over that person's body. And I hardly ever really want to do it, so I don't need to learn how to bring it out."

Emily gazed at her curiously. "Really? You're never tempted to live someone else's life for a while?"

"Like whose?" Amanda asked.

"I don't know . . ." Emily considered this. "Okay, Lady Gaga. I bet she's got a pretty fabulous life."

Amanda sniffed. "I'd rather make my own life fabulous."

Madame's eyes swept the room and settled on another student. "Sarah, do you think this discussion is a waste of time?"

Amanda was actually curious to hear the girl's response.

Of all the classmates, Sarah talked the least about her gift.

The girl with the curly dark hair and the heart-shaped face spoke softly. "I think it's dangerous, Madame."

"How do you mean?" Madame asked.

"If we have total control of our gifts, if we could use them whenever we wanted to, we could end up doing bad things."

Madame gazed at her thoughtfully. "Can you give us an example?"

Everyone turned to look at Sarah, and there was real curiosity in their expressions. Amanda knew why. Supposedly, Sarah had the most powerful gift of all—she could make people do whatever she wanted them to do. None of them had seen much evidence of this remarkable gift, but they knew she had it.

But Sarah didn't use herself as an example. "Well, take Martin, for example. If he could call on his power whenever he wanted to . . ." Her voice trailed off.

"Go on, Sarah," Madame encouraged her.

With clear reluctance, the girl continued. "Maybe . . . maybe Martin doesn't like someone. So he . . . he makes something fall on that person's head and kills him."

"I wouldn't do that," Martin said indignantly.

"Are you sure about that?" Sarah asked. "I mean, what if someone was really, truly getting on your nerves?"

"You're not talking about Martin," Jenna said suddenly. "You're worried about yourself."

"Jenna!" Madame snapped.

Jenna sank back in her seat. "Sorry."

Tracey looked confused as she turned toward Sarah. "Are you afraid Martin is going to drop something on *your* head?"

"No," Sarah said. She looked at her watch and fidgeted, which struck Amanda as very unusual. Sarah was famous for being the perfect student who never behaved inappropriately in any classroom.

Madame glanced at the clock on the wall. "We only have a few more minutes. For tomorrow's class, I want you all to think about this: if you had complete control over your gift, how could you use them in positive ways? How could you help people, maybe even use your gifts to benefit mankind?" She gave them a moment to jot down the assignment.

"Now, does anyone have anything to say before the bell rings?"

Emily raised her hand. "Do you know how Carter is doing at Harmony House?"

Amanda was mildly curious about that, too. Their former classmate had been sent to the institution for troubled teenagers more than a week ago.

Madame nodded. "I've been talking to Doctor Paley regularly. Carter hasn't spoken, but he's cooperating. Doctor Paley believes that eventually he'll be able to make a real connection with him. Oh, and I should tell you, he's not allowed any visitors yet."

Jenna snorted. "Who'd want to visit him? The guy was spying on us! He was consorting with the enemy. As far as I'm concerned, he can spend the rest of his life at Harmony House in solitary confinement."

"Try to keep an open mind about Carter," Madame urged her. "We don't know what his real intentions were."

The bell rang and Madame dismissed them. Amanda took her time gathering up her things, but all the while she kept an eye on Ken. He had already gotten up and was on his way to the door. The big question was— would he be waiting for her outside the class?

He'd been there yesterday when she emerged, and he'd

walked her to her locker. If he did this today, she was going to ask him if he wanted to come home with her for a snack.

He was there! And as soon as she arrived, he began walking by her side.

"Do you think Carter knew what he was doing when he was reporting on the class to Serena?" he asked as they strolled down the hall.

Amanda shrugged. "Who knows?"

Ken finished the comment for her. "And who cares? You know, this class is really starting to annoy me."

"No kidding," Amanda said with feeling. "I mean, what are we really getting out of it?"

Ken nodded. "I'm no better at stopping the voices than I was before. And I sure don't want to invite any more dead people to talk to me."

"And I don't want to be Lady Gaga," Amanda declared. "Personally, I think she looks kind of sleazy."

"And what Madame said about doing something good with our gifts—okay, maybe for some of the others that could work. But the best thing that ever came out of my gift was helping that kid find the lottery ticket his father had hidden before he died—and that was just a fluke. It's not going to happen again."

"We don't belong in that class, Ken," Amanda said.

"I know," Ken said. "But how are we going to get out of it?"

This was the perfect opportunity to invite him over to her place to discuss the matter. But they were approaching her locker now, and Amanda's heart sank when she saw Nina standing there, obviously waiting for her.

It was a funny thing about Nina. She'd been part of Amanda's clique since forever, but she wasn't exactly a friend. What was that word she'd heard on *Gossip Girl*? *Frenemy*. That's what Nina was. They hung out together, but Amanda didn't trust her.

Still, she forced a thin smile to greet the girl. "Hi, what's up?"

"My mom's picking me up to go to the mall. Want to come?"

Amanda groaned inwardly. If she said "yes," she couldn't invite Ken over. If she said "no," she'd have to give Nina an excuse, that she already had plans—which meant she couldn't invite Ken over.

"Yeah, okay," she said without much enthusiasm. She opened her locker.

"How ya doing, Ken?" Nina asked.

"Okay," Ken said.

"I was just thinking about you," Nina went on.

"Yeah? Why?"

Nina shook her head sadly. "Meadowbrook's soccer team is so pitiful this season. They'd be doing so much better if you were still playing."

Ken gave her a modest smile. "I don't know about that. I wish I could play, but I can't get the medical clearance. Because of my ankle."

"Ken was in a bad accident in September," Amanda told Nina.

"I know, I remember," Nina said, glancing at her briefly. Then she turned her full attention back to Ken. "I was so worried about you."

Ken seemed surprised. "Yeah?"

Amanda was more than surprised. Nina had never said one word about Ken's accident. She eyed Nina suspiciously. Was she flirting? And what was that flush spreading across Ken's face? Was he *enjoying* this? She slammed her locker door shut.

"I'm ready," she said shortly. "Let's go. See ya, Ken."

"Bye, Ken," Nina said. She linked her arm through Amanda's arm. Amanda turned her head to give Ken a private, parting smile, but he'd already turned in the opposite direction. What was he thinking after that little encounter? she wondered.

She could certainly see where Jenna's gift could come in handy . . .

CHAPTER THREE

ON TUESDAY MORNING, CARTER woke up. He got out of bed, he went to the sink, he filled the cup and watered the plant. He brushed his teeth, he got dressed, and he went to the dining room. He ate his breakfast, he watched the clock, and when the time was right, he went to Dr. Paley's office.

"Good morning, Carter." The doctor's back was to the boy as he adjusted the video camera. "I want to try something new with you today." He turned to face Carter. "There is a procedure in which a sleeplike condition is induced in the subject. In this condition, the subject is highly susceptible to the suggestions of the doctor. This condition is called hypnosis."

Carter stiffened. He knew that word. That word could make bad things happen. Dr. Paley's eyebrows went up.

"Ah, I see that word disturbs you, and I think I know why. Serena Hancock used hypnosis to make you talk. But it's possible that what Serena used was a counter-hypnosis process. Let me explain my theory."

He pulled out the chair that he normally sat on from behind the desk and placed it in the center of the room. Then he turned the chair that Carter always sat in to face it, and he motioned for Carter to sit down.

Carter didn't move. His entire body seemed to be on alert.

"Sit down, Carter," Dr. Paley said firmly.

He had to obey. He had no choice. Carter sat down.

"This is my theory," Dr. Paley said. "You may believe that Serena hypnotized you, but I believe that you are currently functioning in a state of trauma, and she was able to bring you *out* of that state. That's why you were able to communicate with her."

He leaned back in his chair and studied Carter thoughtfully. "I don't know how she was able to do this. I have tried to locate her, but she seems to have disappeared or changed her name. So what I would like to do is try my own form of hypnosis on you, with the hope that I can somehow cause your current state of hypnosis to end.

I know this all sounds very confusing, but you must trust me. Carter? Carter, what are you looking at?"

Carter had been distracted by a sudden movement. It came from the far corner of the office where a filing cabinet stood. Dr. Paley followed the direction of Carter's eyes.

"Oh, no," the doctor snapped. He got up, grabbed a book from his desk, and tossed it in that direction. A very small mouse retreated behind the cabinet.

"Mice," the doctor murmured. "They're all over the building. I've complained, but it's an old structure and there are bound to be holes in the walls . . . Now, where were we? Ah, yes, I was about to attempt hypnotic therapy." He returned to his seat facing Carter.

"Let's begin." From his shirt pocket he withdrew what looked like a pen, but when he clicked it, a small white light appeared. "I want you to look at this light."

Carter looked at the light.

"The subject is looking at the light," Dr. Paley said quietly. Carter knew he was speaking for the recording device. Dr. Paley recorded or videotaped all the sessions.

Then, in a normal voice, Dr. Paley continued. "Now,

don't take your eyes from the light, but listen to my voice very carefully. I want you to empty your mind. Your mind is like a room full of furniture. The pieces of furniture are your thoughts. I want you to pack your thoughts in boxes, one by one, and take them out of the room."

Carter didn't feel comfortable. Boxes . . . The image bothered him. A sensation began to creep over him. It wasn't hunger, it wasn't cold . . . but something else, something just as disturbing. He knew this sensation but he couldn't put a name to it.

But he did as he was told. He took a thought: Harmony House. He put it in a plain brown box. He carried the thought out of his mind. Then he did the same with the gifted class, the Granger home, and the house where he had met Serena and the other people.

"I'm going to count back from ten," Dr. Paley said. "Close your eyes. You will feel yourself getting sleepy. When I reach the number one, you will be in a deep sleep, but you will continue to hear my voice. Ten . . . nine . . . eight . . . seven . . ."

Carter searched his mind. It was empty—every thought had been packed up and taken out. There hadn't been that much there in the first place. But was he getting sleepy? He didn't think so.

". . . three . . . two . . . one. You are now in a deep sleep and you will do as I say."

Carter knew he wasn't asleep, but it was easy to follow Dr. Paley's commands.

"Raise your right hand. Put your right hand down. Raise your left hand. Put your left hand down. Very good. The subject appears to be in a trance. Now, Carter, let's bring up a memory."

This wouldn't be so easy. Memories were thoughts, and all his thoughts had been removed. But he continued to listen.

"Let's go back to the day you were discovered, on Carter Street. It's night, and you're huddled in a doorway. A policeman finds you. He asks you questions. You don't answer him. You're feeling something, Carter. What are you feeling? Maybe you're lonely. Maybe you're sad."

Lonely . . . sad . . . He couldn't connect to those words.

"Cold . . ." Dr. Paley suggested.

Yes . . . *yes*! He knew that sensation. The chill of the night crept over him, and he was very uncomfortable.

"The subject appears to be shivering," Dr. Paley

murmured. "Carter . . . perhaps you haven't eaten in a while. So you are hungry. Are you hungry, Carter?" After a moment, he said, "The subject is licking his lips."

Cold, hungry, cold, hungry . . . This was bad. Carter didn't want to be there.

"And something else, too, Carter. You're feeling something else. Are you afraid?"

Afraid, afraid, afraid . . . The words rang in his ears, and suddenly all those thoughts he'd pushed out of his head came rushing back in, and more, more thoughts, thoughts he didn't know he had, horrible thoughts . . . Yes, that was the sensation he couldn't remember. He was afraid, and it was horrible, terrible, he had to shut it out, turn it off, go away, go far, far away, to a place where he wouldn't be cold or hungry or frightened . . .

Images, sounds, they flashed across his mind so rapidly, he couldn't identify anything . . . Lights and noises, lights and noises, they went on and on and on, louder and brighter, and the sensation grew stronger . . . Hunger, cold, fear—he had to make them stop! But he couldn't make them stop, so he had to escape. There was a way: he did it before, he could do it again . . .

"Carter. Carter! I'm going to count to ten, and when

I reach ten, you will wake up. One, two, three . . ."

With the doctor's voice, the lights and the noises began to change. Colors faded, and the sounds were softer. Slowly, all became silent and gray again. Safe.

Carter opened his eyes. He didn't understand what had just happened to him, and he looked at Dr. Paley in bewilderment.

Dr. Paley was looking at him with an odd expression, too. As if he'd just seen something he'd never seen before.

"Carter. How do you feel?"

Pain . . . There was pain . . . Carter put his hands to his head in an effort to squeeze out the pain.

"You'd better go back to your room and lie down for a while," Dr. Paley said.

Carter rose and went to the door.

"But I want to see you again later today," Dr. Paley told him. "After I've had a chance to study the videotape and talk to some colleagues. This is very important, Carter. Do you understand me?"

Carter turned his head and looked back at the doctor. Dr. Paley smiled.

"You see, Carter . . . You, too, have a gift."

CHAPTER FOUR

AS AMANDA APPROACHED room 209, she spotted Nina lingering just outside the door of the class.

"What are you doing here?" she asked her "frenemy."

Nina fluttered a thin strip of paper in the air. "You left this in my mother's car yesterday. It must have fallen out of your bag."

Amanda took the paper and examined it. It was the receipt for a pair of shoes she'd bought at the mall the day before.

"You'll need this if you want to return the shoes," Nina pointed out.

"I love those sandals, I'm not going to take them back," Amanda replied. Then she frowned. "Why are you giving me this now? Why didn't you give it to me at lunch today?"

Nina smiled sweetly. "I forgot."

Amanda doubted that. Nina knew that Ken was in this class with Amanda. She was just looking for an excuse to hang out in front of the room and "accidentally" run into him.

"Thanks," she said, tossing the receipt in her bag. "Bye."

But just as she suspected, Nina remained by the door. From her seat in class, Amanda could see Ken arrive and Nina stopping him. They weren't able to talk long—the bell was about to ring—but Amanda fumed anyway.

She knew she shouldn't be surprised. Ken was a highly desirable guy, popular and good-looking. And Nina had always competed with Amanda for everything from leadership of their clique to being the first with the current "It" purse, so why not with boys, too? It was only natural that Nina would go after the same one Amanda wanted.

Nina knew that Amanda was interested in Ken. Ever since he'd kissed her underwater at a pool party last summer, she'd had feelings for him. (Okay, the kiss was the result of a dare from some other guys, but even so, it *was* a kiss.) In her efforts to get a relationship going,

Amanda had had ups and downs, but right now, things seemed to be going well. There was no way she'd let Nina intrude.

She flashed her most brilliant smile at Ken as he took his seat, but there was no opportunity to talk. Madame called for everyone's attention.

"Yesterday, I asked you to think about how you could use your gifts in positive ways. Does anyone have any thoughts on the subject?"

Charles spoke. "I've done that. I got the gun away from that woman Clare, when she had Emily in her car."

"Yes, I remember," Madame said. "But I'm interested in discussing how you can help others—not just the people in this class, but society in general."

Martin piped up. "You mean, like a superhero? If I could get a handle on my power whenever I wanted, I could run around saving people from bullies."

"Let's not jump that far ahead," Madame cautioned. "I'm not telling you to become superheroes. We're just trying to explore the potential of your gifts. If you did have control, you might have opportunities to benefit mankind."

Emily had a question. "But how? Like, what if I had a vision of a plane crashing and I called the airline to warn them? They'd want to know how I knew about it."

"What good would it do anyway?" Jenna asked. "They wouldn't believe you."

"And if they did believe you," Tracey chimed in, "you'd be revealing your gift. Which we're not supposed to do." She looked at Madame. "Right?"

Amanda was mildly surprised that Madame didn't make her usual quick response to that question. The teacher actually seemed uncertain. Finally, she spoke.

"There may be situations where you will be able to safely reveal yourselves," she said slowly, "to certain people, and under certain conditions. But that's not what I want us to discuss now. At this point in time, I want you to think about ways in which you could use your gifts discreetly. To help people without calling attention to yourselves."

What's the point of that? Amanda wondered. *We wouldn't get any credit for our good deeds.*

Jenna suddenly burst out laughing. Madame looked startled.

"What's so funny about that, Jenna?" she demanded to know.

"Sorry, Madame. But I was just trying to imagine Amanda doing a good deed when she wouldn't get any credit for it."

"She was reading my mind, Madame!" Amanda complained. Then she realized she'd just affirmed what Jenna had said, and she sank back in her chair. From the corner of her eye she could see Ken looking at her, and it wasn't exactly in admiration. Did he really think she was the kind of person who would never do anything for anyone else?

Madame was angry. "Jenna, how many times do I need to remind you? You have absolutely no right to eavesdrop on your classmates' thoughts! It's rude, and you're invading their privacy."

"But I wasn't reading her mind," Jenna protested. "It was my own thought."

Liar, Amanda thought. And she didn't care if Jenna heard her.

Tracey spoke. "Jenna, you're not being fair. Remember when Amanda was in my head? She did a lot of nice things for me."

"Yeah, because she was afraid she was stuck being you forever," Jenna retorted. "Look, all I'm saying is that Amanda won't ever be a superhero. She's too selfish."

Madame was losing patience. "Could we please get back to the subject? Charles . . . can you think of a way you could use your gift discreetly to help people?"

Charles thought about it. "Okay, what about this? I'm in a grocery store, and there's this little old man who wants to buy a can of soup. Only it's on a really high shelf and he can't reach it. So when he's not looking, I make the can of soup come off the shelf and into his shopping basket."

Martin looked at him scornfully. "You think getting a can of soup off a shelf benefits mankind?"

Ken had a problem with this, too. "And when the old man sees the can in his basket and he doesn't know how it got there, he'll be afraid he's losing *his* mind."

Madame smiled. "It was a positive thought, Charles, but you can see there are ramifications and consequences to every action. Sarah, you haven't spoken. Do you have a comment to make?"

"No, Madame," Sarah said.

"For this class, I asked you to think about how you

could use your gift in a positive way. Did you do this?"

"No, Madame."

Amanda was shocked. She'd had other classes with Sarah, and the girl was widely known as Little Miss Perfect who always did what teachers told her to do. It was weird that she would actually not do the assignment. Amanda herself hadn't done the assignment either, but if Madame asked, she would say that she'd thought and thought about it but hadn't been able to come up with an example. Sarah was such a goody-goody, she wasn't even capable of lying!

"Well, Sarah, think about it now." Madame's tone was kind but firm. "You have a very powerful gift. More than anyone else here, you have the ability to help people. Sarah, are you listening?"

Sarah had lowered her head, and no one could see her face. "Yes, Madame."

"Then answer me. What could you do to benefit mankind?"

"I can't," Sarah replied in an almost inaudible whisper.

"Why not?"

Sarah raised her head, and now Amanda could see tears streaming down her face. "I can't, Madame. I can't!"

Amanda was taken aback. The girl looked and sounded unbelievably upset, like she was on the verge of a nervous breakdown or something. It was awful. Amanda could feel her pain . . .

Uh-oh, this was dangerous! Quickly she concentrated on coming up with another emotional reaction. Silly girl, why is she freaking out? What a wimp . . .

But now Sarah was sobbing hysterically, and Amanda couldn't drown out the sound. She had to make this stop before pity overwhelmed her.

"Leave her alone," she said loudly. "She hasn't done anything wrong. She's doesn't have to benefit mankind if she doesn't want to!"

"You would say that," Jenna declared. "You're so selfish, Amanda!"

Madame hurried over to Sarah and put a hand on her shoulder. "Sarah, you need to calm down."

But Sarah continued to cry, and Madame turned to Emily. "Could you take Sarah to the infirmary, Emily?"

"Sure," Emily said. She got up and went to Sarah's desk. "Come on, Sarah."

Still sobbing, Sarah rose from her desk and left the room with Emily.

For a moment, the room was silent. Then Martin asked, "Why does she get so upset when we ask about her gift, Madame?"

Before Madame had a chance to reply, the chiming of three bells sounded from the intercom. It was followed by the voice of the school secretary.

"Madame, could you come to the office, please?"

Madame sighed and went to the door. "Class, continue discussing positive ways in which you can use your gifts," she ordered them before walking out.

Naturally, everyone started talking about anything but that.

"Do you think Carter is telling that doctor all about us?" Charles asked.

"He can't talk," Martin pointed out.

"But he *can*," Tracey piped up. "Remember? I told you guys—I saw him talking to that Serena."

Amanda didn't care what Carter was doing. She was

more concerned about what Ken might be thinking after that little exchange with Jenna. Did he think she was selfish, too?

"Ken . . ."

He was staring straight ahead, and he didn't seem to have heard her. Or maybe he was intentionally ignoring her. Nervously, she nudged him. "*Ken.*"

He turned. "Oh, sorry. I was listening to someone."

Immediately, she turned on her most sympathetic expression. "A dead person?"

He nodded. "You remember that sweet old lady I told you about? The one who was hooked on a soap opera before she died?"

She didn't remember, but she nodded anyway.

"She wanted to know what happened in the last episode."

It came back to her. "Oh, right. You've been watching it for her." She wrinkled her nose. "Isn't that a drag? I mean, it's a really stupid show."

"Yeah, it's awful. But it meant a lot to her."

"Well, you're doing a good deed, I guess," Amanda said. "Are dead people still considered part of mankind?"

Tracey interrupted their private conversation. "Ken, what do you think?"

"About what?" Ken asked.

"Carter. Do you think he's talking about us?"

"He might be telling the doctor," Ken suggested.

"I'm not worried about that," Jenna said. "Doctor Paley's a good guy. He already knows about me. And Madame wouldn't be talking to him every day if she didn't trust him. But there are a lot of creepy people living at Harmony House. Serious losers, kids with bad connections. I hope he's not talking to them."

"Yeah, I wish I knew what was going on over there," Charles commented. "Too bad he's not allowed to have any visitors."

Martin turned to Jenna. "Couldn't *you* get into the place? They know you there."

Jenna shook her head. "Doesn't make any difference— they're really strict. There's a guard who won't let anyone past the reception area unless they've got a pass."

"I could get in!" Tracey declared. "The guard wouldn't see me if I'm invisible. I could follow Carter around and find out what he's up to."

"Forget it," Jenna said. "Remember what happened

when you tried to spy on him before? And you became visible again? No offense, Tracey—I know you're improving, but you just don't have enough control of your gift. You could get into serious trouble if you're caught there."

"I've got an idea," Martin said.

Jenna rolled her eyes. "Let me guess. You'll punch out the guard."

"Jenna, don't tease him," Tracey hissed.

But Martin really did seem to be developing some control. "I'm thinking Amanda could get in."

Aghast, Amanda turned to him. "Me?"

"Like Jenna said, the place is full of losers," Martin said. "There's got to be someone checking in who you could feel sorry for. You could do your bodysnatching thing, take over, and go in as that person."

Amanda stared at him in horror. What kind of insane idea was that? Then she caught Ken's eye. He was looking at her with interest.

"You think you could do that?"

"She could," Jenna broke in, "but she wouldn't. Do you really think Amanda's going to do something to help us?"

Amanda swallowed hard. "Don't speak for me, Jenna. I could try . . ."

"Today?" Jenna asked.

"Um . . . let me think . . . I don't even know where Harmony House is . . ."

"I'll take you there," Jenna declared. "Right after class."

That was definitely admiration on Ken's face. Amanda swallowed again and smiled thinly.

"Great."

CHAPTER FIVE

THE PAIN IN HIS head was gone by the time Carter returned to Dr. Paley's office. Even so, something in his head was different. It was like the TV in his dreams was embedded somewhere in his brain. At some point during the last session, it had been turned on. It was off again now, and Carter preferred this state of mind. Now that he was entering Dr. Paley's office, he had the sensation it could be turned on again, and he didn't want that. But he'd been told to return, and he did what he was told.

Dr. Paley seemed different, too. His eyes were brighter, and his smile was wider. Change meant danger. Carter began to shiver.

"Sit down, Carter. I want to show you something." He wheeled a trolley to the middle of the room and positioned it in front of Carter's chair. On top of the trolley stood a television, smaller than the one in his dreams, but still a television. Carter felt his heartbeat quicken.

Dr. Paley didn't notice his discomfort. "I want to show you the tape I made of our session this morning." He touched a button and slipped a disk into an opening. Then he sat down behind his desk, where he, too, could see the screen. He held a remote control toward the TV, it flickered to life, and Carter saw himself, sitting in this same chair. He couldn't see Dr. Paley on the screen, but he heard his voice.

"I'm going to count back from ten," Dr. Paley said. "Close your eyes. You will feel yourself getting sleepy. When I reach the number one, you will be in a deep sleep, but you will continue to hear my voice. Ten . . . nine . . . eight . . . seven . . ."

The pain was coming back. Carter covered his ears. Quickly, Dr. Paley took the remote control. The tape continued, but Carter didn't hear anything.

"Actually, we don't need the sound," Dr. Paley said. "You never spoke. Now, watch carefully, Carter. Here it comes."

Carter didn't have any expectations as to what he might have done under the spell of the doctor's hypnosis, but even so, it was a shock to see himself get smaller and smaller.

Dr. Paley had said Carter had a gift. Was it a gift like Tracey's? Then he realized that the chair on the screen wasn't vacant. A small white rabbit sat there, twitching its nose.

"That's not really a rabbit, Carter," Dr. Paley said softly. "That's you."

He picked up the remote control. "I'm going to fast-forward for a minute. There, now watch this."

The rabbit on the chair seemed to puff up. Then it became fuzzy, almost impossible to identify as a rabbit. As it enlarged, it changed form. The form became too blurry to see anything in detail, but then Carter could see the outline of arms, legs, a torso . . . The focus returned. It was Carter, in the same position as before, still sitting in his chair. And all this happened in less than a second.

"You're suffering from Acute Faculative Allomorphy, Carter, commonly known as shapeshifting," Dr. Paley said.

Carter took his eyes off the screen and looked at the doctor. His whole body began to tremble.

Dr. Paley came out from behind his desk and drew another chair closer to Carter. He placed a warm hand gently on Carter's shoulder.

"Don't get upset, Carter. You're going to be all right. You're safe here. Nobody is going to hurt you. As I told you this morning, you have a gift. It's a very unusual gift—very few cases have been recorded, and these cases have been kept secret. My own interest in extraordinary abilities has given me access to information that has long been hidden from the public."

His voice was calming, and Carter stopped shaking. But was he really safe? How could he be sure?

The doctor continued. "You must know by now that uncommon gifts like this exist. Think about your classmates."

Carter stiffened. He could hear Madame's voice. "Never tell, never tell." He'd told Serena, and he'd been sent away from the class.

It was almost as if Dr. Paley could read his thoughts. "You're not in trouble, Carter. No one is going to hurt you, or any of your classmates. I know everything because I've been talking with Madame. She has always suspected that you, too, may have some kind of special ability. We both have your best interests at heart. We want to help you."

The words rang true, and Carter had always trusted Madame.

"I've learned from Madame that many of your classmates' gifts arose through extreme situations—a trauma, a crisis of some sort—and I believe this may be true of you, too. We need to know why you became a shape shifter. From your reaction in watching the tape I could see you were shocked, but I don't think that was the first time you've ever shifted. Your state of amnesia has erased all memories of your gift. But the explanation for your ability is buried deep within your subconscious. I can't reach you through traditional hypnotic procedures, so I need to try something else."

Carter's eyes followed the doctor as he rose and went to the white cabinet in the corner of the room. He opened a drawer.

"I'm going to give you an injection. It's perfectly safe—it's just a sedative that will help you relax completely and allow you to overcome the inhibitions that are preventing you from speaking. Hopefully, you will recover some memories and be able to tell me about your past. Would you roll up your sleeve, please?"

It was a direct order. Carter had to obey. But Dr. Paley must have sensed the fear that engulfed him, because his voice became even more soothing.

"You'll only feel a little prick, and retrieving the memories shouldn't be painful. You may not even remember what you tell me. But I'm taping you so you'll be able to watch it all later. I'm keeping no secrets from you. You have to trust me, and you must not fight the need to express yourself."

It was just as Dr. Paley said—the injection was just a little sting in his arm, and then he felt nothing.

"We're going back in time, to six months ago. Close your eyes, Carter."

Carter closed his eyes, but what he saw wasn't darkness. At first he thought he was dreaming, because he could see the boy of his dreams. But then it was as if he was inside the boy, and it wasn't a dream. The boy was him.

He looked around, and everything he saw was familiar and comforting. The room held a sofa, two armchairs, a bookcase. At one end of the room, there was a large wooden table and chairs. On the floor, there was a colorful rug. There were windows, and through the windows he could see flowers.

He knew this house. He knew about things he couldn't even see, like the basketball hoop over the two-car garage. He knew that through the archway there was a big kitchen. He knew that if he went past the table and through another archway he'd be in a hallway, and off the hallway were three bedrooms. One of those bedrooms belonged to him.

Someone was singing. He could hear a woman's voice drifting out from another room. He knew the voice. It belonged to his mother.

A man sat in one of the armchairs with a newspaper in his hands. He knew this man. He was called "Dad."

The man looked at him. "I'm sorry, Paul. It's just not possible."

Paul. That was the boy's name. Not Carter. Paul.

My name is Paul.

He knew what his father was talking about, too. Paul had just asked him if they could buy one of the puppies that had been born to their neighbor's dog.

"But it's so tiny, Dad. And Mrs. Robbins says he won't get much bigger."

His father smiled, but he shook his head. "Your mother is allergic to dog hair, Paul. It wouldn't matter whether the dog was big or small. Your mother can't visit the Robbinses' house for more than a few minutes. If we had a dog living in this house, even if you kept him in your room, she'd get sick. You wouldn't want that."

"No," Paul said. He turned to see his mother standing in the archway.

"I'm so sorry, sweetie-pie," she said. That was her special name for him, "sweetie-pie." He was grateful for the fact that she never used it when any of his friends were around. Not that he had many friends, not yet. They'd just moved here a few weeks ago.

They moved a lot. Every now and then, serious men came to talk to his parents. Soon after that, they would move. Years ago, Paul had asked his father who the men were and why they were always moving. His father told him that the men were from the government, and they were protecting them. They were part of something called a "witness protection program." His parents had witnessed a crime, and so had Paul, even though he couldn't remember it. He'd only been four at the time.

But ever since then they all had to be protected from the criminals, who had never been caught. His parents told Paul they had nothing to worry about as long as they did what the government men told them to do. And Paul didn't worry, because he trusted his father and his mother.

Right now, though, his mother looked a little worried. But it had nothing to do with criminals.

"Sweetie-pie, I hope you don't hate me for this," she said.

"I don't hate you, Mom," Paul replied.

"I'm going to see a specialist next week," she told him. "Maybe there's a new medicine for my allergy."

"Thanks, Mom," Paul said. "But it's okay, I don't have to have a dog. How about a couple of gerbils?"

"That might be just fine," his mother said. "I'll ask the doctor." She looked at her watch. "I need to run to the grocery store before dinner. Paul, could you empty the dishwasher?"

"Sure." He went into the kitchen. Just as he opened the dishwasher door, he heard a knock on the front door. His mother must have opened it, because he heard her cry out.

"What do you want?"

Then his father's voice: "What do you think you're doing?"

And then a horrible loud bang, followed by the sound of a body falling down. Then another bang, and another body hit the floor.

A gruff voice muttered, "We gotta find the kid."

Paul heard the footsteps coming down the hall. He knew they wouldn't find anyone in the bedrooms, and the next place they'd look would be the kitchen. Frantically, he looked around for a place to hide.

He ran into the little pantry and shut the door. But there was no lock to keep the men from opening it, and he could hear them coming.

His parents couldn't help him. There was no escape. In seconds the men would open the door and shoot him, just as they had shot his mother and his father. Danger— he was in terrible danger. There had to be some way, *some way* to save himself. If only he could become invisible . . .

He couldn't. But he could do something else. He didn't know he could do it—it just happened, and when it did, it felt like the most completely natural reaction he could have to the situation.

And when one of the men pulled open the door to the pantry, he didn't see Paul. He couldn't even see the small gerbil hiding behind a box of cereal.

From way off in the distance came the sound of sirens.

"The neighbors must have heard the shots," a man said. "Let's get out of here."

From behind the box, Paul waited until he couldn't hear any voices. Then, slowly, he crept out of the pantry.

How odd the kitchen suddenly seemed to him. Such a big space . . . he knew he could scamper across it but he was afraid to move too quickly. He could imagine the sight he would encounter in the living room, and he wasn't ready for that. He wasn't ready for anything. Huge structures loomed ominously over him. He knew what they were—a refrigerator, a dishwasher—but his perspective made them frightening. He inched his way across the cold linoleum floor, and he'd almost reached the archway when the door to the living room burst open.

Frantically, he ran behind the stove. Peering out, he saw men in police uniforms. They were holding guns.

If he ran out the way he was, would they shoot him? He couldn't turn back into himself, not while he was behind the stove—he wouldn't fit into the space, he'd be crushed. And if he ran out and then transformed, the police might think he was one of the bad guys and kill him.

He heard one of them speak. "We need an ambulance immediately."

Enormous boot-clad feet were directly in front of him. "Kitchen's clear," a voice rang out.

Another voice. "Bedrooms and bathroom are clear."

And then another voice. "It looks bad. I'm not getting a pulse on either of them."

Paul knew whom they were talking about.

He stayed where he was. Time passed. There were new voices, new sounds.

"The house wasn't ransacked. This doesn't look like a burglary. Someone had it in for these folks."

"They must have been pros. We're not going to find any fingerprints."

"Headquarters says don't touch anything. They're calling in the FBI."

"Why?"

"No idea."

"Can we move the bodies?"

"Yeah."

Bodies. Paul knew what that meant. His parents were dead.

He remained behind the stove, and he had no idea how long he was there. There were more voices, more sounds. And then, finally, there was silence.

He came out and moved into the living room. There were some dark stains on the carpet, and he sniffed them. Blood. His parents' blood. Vaguely, he wondered why he wasn't crying. Maybe gerbils couldn't cry.

And now what was he supposed to do?

CHAPTER SIX

WHEN MADAME returned to the class, she was visibly excited.

"Good news, class! I've just had a conversation with Doctor Paley. Carter has had a breakthrough. He's talking!"

"What's he saying?" Tracey asked.

"He's just beginning to remember who he is, where he came from. Doctor Paley couldn't talk long, so I don't have any details yet."

"Is he talking about us?" Jenna wanted to know.

"Doctor Paley didn't say." Madame's eyes swept the room. "Class, I know you're all concerned, not only for Carter but for your own safety as well. And I can understand that. But Doctor Paley is a medical person, a specialist. He accepts the possibilities of abilities that cannot be explained by science. He is a man of integrity. I trust him, and I believe he can help us."

Jenna wasn't satisfied with that. "But what if Carter starts talking to other people at Harmony House? Some of the kids who stay there are bad news."

The bell rang. "I'll bring this concern up with Doctor Paley," Madame promised as she dismissed them.

As she rose from her desk, Amanda was hoping that Jenna might have forgotten about their afterschool plans. No such luck. Jenna made it to the doorway first and practically blocked Amanda from leaving.

"Let's go."

"I need to stop by my locker," Amanda protested. She didn't really, but she'd do anything to postpone this adventure. She had a sudden inspiration. "I'll meet you by the back entrance."

Jenna looked at her skeptically, but she nodded and took off. Ken joined Amanda, and they walked together to her locker.

"That's really cool, what you're doing," Ken said. "Are you scared?"

"A little nervous," Amanda admitted. "I don't know if it'll work. And even if I can take someone over, I always worry about being able to get back into myself."

"Want me to come along with you guys?"

Of course she would have loved to have him come along, but she knew it wasn't a good idea. Jenna would only entertain him with tales of Amanda's selfishness.

She smiled sweetly. "It's so nice of you to offer, Ken. But if you're there, it might make it harder for me to take over someone."

"Why?"

This was risky, but she had to take a chance. She lowered her eyes demurely. "Because I have to concentrate really hard to do it. And if you're there . . . well, it might be hard to concentrate on anyone else."

Was she coming on too strong? She cast a sidelong glance at him. It was hard to say, but she could swear she saw a little blush creep up his face. Then he smiled. Unfortunately, he wasn't looking at her anymore.

"Hi, Nina."

And there she was, the frenemy, waiting by Amanda's locker. Like a cat waiting for a mouse and ready to pounce.

Nina acted like she was happy to see both of them, but Amanda knew a performance when she saw one.

"Hi, guys!" Nina chirped. "Have you seen how nice

it is outside? It's like summer! I am so totally up for an ice cream. Who wants to come with me?"

Amanda rolled her eyes. Nina never ate ice cream. She was one of those idiots who never consumed anything nice for fear it might add an ounce to her scrawny frame.

And to make matters worse, Jenna chose that precise moment to appear. "Are you ready to go?" she asked Amanda.

Amanda should have known Jenna wouldn't wait long by the back door. She was probably worried Amanda would sneak out of the front entrance—which was exactly what she had been considering.

Nina, of course, was staring at Jenna with her mouth open. Amanda didn't have to be a mind reader to know what was going on in her so-called friend's head. The notorious goth girl had plans with Queen Beeson?

"Class project," Amanda offered by way of explanation. She raised her hand in a casual salute to the others. But inside she was tormented as she left Ken alone with Nina to get ice cream.

Was Nina really a threat? Okay, she was cute, but

Amanda knew she herself was cuter. Looks weren't everything, though. And Nina did have something Amanda didn't have. Nina was normal. She didn't have any weird gift to deal with. Ken wanted to be normal. Would he be intrigued with the notion of hanging out with a normal girl?

Of course she said nothing about this to Jenna. Not that Jenna would care. As soon as they were out of the building, she started to give instructions.

"We'll take the bus to City Hall and walk from there. There are usually three or four new admissions to Harmony House every day, and we can check them out in the reception area."

"Whatever," Amanda mumbled. They crossed the street and went to the bus stop.

Jenna continued. "It's important that you're very careful about whose body you take over. Boys and girls live in separate sections, so it's best to pick a boy. You'll be able to hang around Carter more. If you're a girl, you'll only be able to see him in the dining hall, the TV room, and the game room. You won't be able to get into Carter's room."

Amanda tried to tune her out. *Blah, blah, blah . . .* She

didn't want to listen to Jenna's instructions. All she could do was concentrate on blocking Jenna from hearing her own thoughts, mainly the thought that she did not want to be doing this at all.

CHAPTER SEVEN

THE BOY FORMERLY KNOWN as Carter Street had been in Dr. Paley's office for hours now. This was the third time he'd watched the video and listened to himself tell his story under hypnosis, but it wasn't getting any easier for him. He still couldn't get used to the sound of his voice. He sounded so normal—even if the story he told wasn't ordinary at all.

"I didn't know where to go. I stayed at home."

From off screen, the voice of Dr. Paley could be heard. "Why did you choose to be a gerbil?"

"It was the first thing that came to my mind, because I'd just asked my mother about getting some gerbils."

"Where you shocked to realize you could do this?"

"No. It felt natural. I had to be something very small to hide."

"How did you survive?" Dr. Paley asked. "Were you able to eat anything?"

"I found some crumbs behind the stove. That was a surprise. My mother was always sweeping the floor."

"Where did you sleep, Paul?"

That name . . . He'd completely forgotten it. It still wasn't familiar, but strangely enough, it sounded right.

"The bottom drawer of my chest of drawers was open. I was able to jump in and sleep on a sweater."

"How long did you stay in the house?"

"I don't know. I couldn't see a clock. I couldn't even tell if it was day or night."

"Why did you leave?"

So many questions . . . Paul watched his own face on the screen. He looked tired, but he kept on talking.

"Some people must have come. I heard them close the drawer of the chest of drawers. I could feel it moving. I couldn't get out. I was in a dark place with no food. I was hungry." He stopped talking, and Paul could see that his body had begun to tremble.

"Keep talking, Paul. What happened next?"

"The chest of drawers stopped moving. It was in another place—a cold place. I got hungrier and colder. Then the drawer was opened. I was weak, but I got out of the drawer. People must have seen me—someone yelled, someone threw something at me. I was surprised. I thought people liked gerbils. They keep them as pets."

"Yes, yes, but perhaps they were startled because they didn't expect to see a gerbil in a storage unit. Then what did you do?"

"I got away. I was outside. But it was still cold, and I was so hungry. I became a boy again."

"And that was when you were found," Dr. Paley said.

"I guess so."

"Why didn't you say anything?"

"I turned myself off."

"What do you mean?"

"Like a TV. I was off."

There was a moment of silence. Then he heard Dr. Paley's voice again, only this time it wasn't from the screen. The real Dr. Paley was in the room, and he'd paused the videotape.

"You've been turned back on now, Paul." The doctor moved his chair so he could be directly facing him. "I've done some research on your family. You were four years old when you and your parents witnessed an act of organized crime in New York—a murder. Your parents testified against the criminals, and that put their lives in danger. Your life was in danger, too. You couldn't testify, but you were still a witness. So the government put your family in a witness protection program. Your name was changed, and you were moved to another city. But the crime syndicate discovered your whereabouts and you were moved again, and then again. You have a memory of many homes, don't you?"

Paul nodded. In his mind he saw a small house, a large house, a hotel, an apartment. He dimly recalled many times when his parents were talking quietly, worriedly, and then abruptly falling silent when he entered the room. They must have tried so hard to keep him from feeling the danger they were all in.

"It wasn't easy tracking you," Dr. Paley continued. "Your name was changed many times. Your birth name was Paul, but you've been called Daniel, Sam, and Jonathan. It was in your last home that your parents went back to your original name, Paul."

So that was why Paul sounded natural, but not familiar. A lot of things were making sense now.

"And your last names—you've been Fletcher,

O'Malley, and Kingston. Do you have a preference for one over the other?"

Paul shook his head.

"Well, I don't want to give you a name that the criminal syndicate might recognize. How about if we call you Paul Carter?"

Paul nodded.

"How do you feel, Paul?"

Feel—the word made more sense now. He could remember feelings. He remembered feeling excited on the roller coaster. He remembered feeling happy when he made it all the way around the baseball diamond. He remembered feeling disappointed when he learned he couldn't have a dog.

And he remembered horror, terror, when those men killed his parents. He remembered feeling frightened.

He was still frightened. He didn't have to speak— Dr. Paley must have read it in his expression.

"You're scared, aren't you?"

Paul nodded.

"You have a gift, Paul," Dr. Paley said. "Just like your classmates. How does that feel, knowing you have a gift?"

It was hard trying to decide what to say about that, and even harder actually saying it. He managed to get some words out. "I . . . don't . . . know."

"Do you feel good?"

That wasn't the word. Paul shook his head.

"Are you afraid of your gift?"

That was closer to what he felt. Paul nodded.

"Don't be," Dr. Paley said. "I can help you."

CHAPTER EIGHT

THE BUS ARRIVED, AND Amanda reluctantly followed Jenna up the steps. Now that they were among other people, Jenna lowered her voice. "Remember to keep an eye on the resident assistants. When I was there, a real goon tried to blackmail me. He's been fired, but there might be other creeps around. Don't trust anyone."

Amanda fumbled in her bag and pulled out her iPod. Without even looking at Jenna, she stuck the plugs in her ears and turned it on. Jenna glared at her, but Amanda closed her eyes.

She wasn't lying when she admitted to Ken that she was a little nervous. She knew she was getting better and better at bodysnatching, but there was always the chance something could go wrong. She could get stuck being a juvenile delinquent forever. But this would definitely impress her classmates. Nobody could call her selfish again.

Quickly, she amended her thoughts. Of course she didn't really care what any of those weirdos thought about her, and the only person she wanted to impress was Ken.

Jenna poked her in the arm when it was time to get off the bus. "Don't do that," Amanda snapped. "I'll get a bruise." Which made her think of something else.

"Do these kids at Harmony House get into physical fights?" she asked nervously. She took the plugs out of her ears.

Jenna shrugged. "The resident assistants break up the fights."

That wasn't much comfort.

"How long does it take for you to get into someone?" Jenna asked.

"That depends," Amanda replied. "If I feel really sorry for someone, if someone's super-pitiful, it can happen pretty quickly."

Jenna looked at her curiously. "You were Sarah for a while, weren't you? How did you make that happen? There's nothing pitiful about Sarah."

Amanda looked at her scornfully. "Are you kidding?

She's a goody-goody. I don't think she knows what fun means. She dresses like a ten-year-old. And have you ever seen her with a boy?"

Jenna met Amanda's scorn with her own scorn. "So what?"

Amanda knew Jenna would never understand, so she didn't even try to explain. "I don't think it will be very difficult for me to take over someone at Harmony House. Considering the kind of people who end up there . . ." She gave Jenna a meaningful look, but Jenna didn't catch it. She was staring at someone across the street.

"Look at that girl," Jenna said.

Amanda gave her a quick once-over. She seemed to be in her mid-teens, average height, with long blond hair and a backpack hanging from her shoulders. What Amanda found most interesting about her were her jeans. She recognized the super-skinny, washed-out style immediately—she'd been thinking about them ever since she saw them in *Seventeen*, and she was waiting for them to show up in one of the local boutiques. Where had that girl found them?

But surely that wasn't what interested Jenna. "What about her?" Amanda asked.

"She's hitchhiking!"

Sure enough, Amanda saw the girl stick out her thumb as a car passed. "That's dangerous."

"No kidding," Jenna said. "She shouldn't get into a car with a stranger."

Amanda shrugged. "Maybe someone nice will pick her up."

Jenna shook her head. "Most people don't stop for hitchhikers. I mean, the hitchhiker could end up being a carjacker or something. It's dangerous for both of them."

"Someone's pulling over for her," Amanda said.

Jenna stared at the driver. Then, under her breath, she swore.

"What's the matter?" Amanda asked.

"I'm getting his thoughts. He thinks she looks hot . . . I don't think he just wants to give her a ride."

From what Amanda could see, the guy in the car looked pretty ordinary, but of course that didn't mean anything. She'd seen enough photos of criminals to know that they could look like perfectly nice people.

Both girls watched as the hitchhiker ambled toward the car.

"We gotta stop her," Jenna declared.

There was no way they could get across the busy street before the girl reached the car. Then Amanda had an idea.

"Wait, I think I can do something." She stared at the hitchhiker. *You stupid idiot, what are you doing? . . .* No, that was scorn, not pity. She tried again.

You poor thing, you have no idea what kind of danger you're in, you're going to suffer . . . Pity for the girl swept over her. She was getting closer to the car now, she was in big trouble . . .

It was a pretty new car, and she recognized the brand from the name on the back fender. The driver wasn't from around there—she could tell by the words on the license plate. She saw all this very clearly because she was there, close enough to touch the car. She had become the hitchhiker.

A man leaned out the window on the driver's side. "Need a ride, honey?"

Amanda-Hitchhiker glared at him grimly. "No, thank you. And I've seen your license plate number, so don't even think about trying to pick up anyone else, because I'm going to—"

She wasn't able to complete her threat. The car sped away.

Well, at least that part of the mission was successful. Now for the next part. Could she get back into herself without too much difficulty?

She looked back to the other side of the road, where Jenna and Other-Amanda were standing, and concentrated on the figure that looked like her.

Me—that's me. She closed her eyes and chanted the words over and over. She visualized herself as she really was, imprinting the image on her mind. And when she opened her eyes, she was thrilled. It worked! She was back in her own body and feeling totally normal. Amazing! She was getting really good at this—she was in complete control of her gift. Or maybe this experience was just a fluke and it wouldn't be as easy next time. Even so, clearly, she'd made real progress.

Not that she really cared, she reminded herself. She was more interested in removing the gift than improving it. But still, at least now she'd feel more confident about taking over someone at Harmony House.

Naturally, there wasn't a word of congratulations from Jenna. She was already halfway across the street, making her way to where the hitchhiker stood. Amanda followed her.

The hitchhiker wore a dazed expression.

"You okay?" Jenna asked.

"I feel a little dizzy," the blond-haired girl murmured. She blinked a couple of times. "Who are you? What happened to my ride?"

"He took off," Jenna said. "You lucked out."

The girl looked at her blankly. "Huh?"

Amanda wasn't about to let Jenna get the credit for this. "Do you have any idea how dangerous hitchhiking is? Didn't your mother ever tell you never to get into a car with a stranger?"

"I don't take advice from *her*," the girl declared. "She just took off with her boyfriend—she doesn't care about me."

That was kind of sad, Amanda thought. She caught herself before she could feel too sorry for the girl. She didn't want to be her again, even if she did have the jeans Amanda craved. "Where are you going?"

"I'm supposed to be spending the week at my dad's."

"You think he'd want you to be hitchhiking?" Jenna asked.

The girl grinned. "Actually, he sent me money to take a taxi. But I spent it on these jeans."

"I can't blame you," Amanda said. "They're fantastic, I love the stitching."

Jenna shot her a withering look. "That was really stupid. You have to take a taxi the rest of the way. I'm sure you can hail one here."

"Glad to," the girl replied. "Only I don't have any money to pay for one."

Jenna fished around in her pocket. "I've got two bucks." She turned to Amanda. "What about you?"

Reluctantly, Amanda took out her wallet. Looking inside, she said, "Five dollars."

Jenna peered into the wallet. "You've got a ten." She pulled it out.

"Hey!" Amanda cried in outrage.

Jenna stepped out in the street and waved her hand in the air. A taxi pulled up, and a moment later the hitch-hiker was safely on her way to her father's.

"I can't believe you stole my money!" Amanda exclaimed.

Jenna just shrugged, but she looked at Amanda with actual interest. "It's funny. I always thought your gift was pretty worthless, but you might have just saved that girl's life."

It was Amanda's turn to shrug, but Jenna had a point. And this would make a very good story to tell Ken. It would certainly top any story Nina might be telling him right now.

Harmony House was just around the next corner. Together the girls went up the driveway and through the wide double doors into the reception area. Amanda had expected to see a room full of lowlife teens, but with the exception of a woman behind a desk, the area was vacant.

"There's no one here," Amanda murmured.

Jenna nodded toward some chairs. "We'll hang around—someone will show up. They get new admissions every day."

But the receptionist was watching them, and before they could sit down, she spoke. "Can I help you girls?"

"We're just waiting for someone," Jenna replied.

"Who?"

Jenna opened her mouth but nothing came out. Amanda looked around. A handsome young uniformed man was coming out of one of the doors that led into the institution.

"Him," she said.

The receptionist looked in the direction Amanda was pointing. "Officer Fisher? These girls want to see you."

The man looked in their direction and smiled. "Jenna!"

Jenna didn't smile back. "Hello. I, uh, I was just visiting someone. I have to go now." And before Amanda's astonished eyes, she hurried out of the building.

"I guess she didn't really want to see me," the man sighed. "Hi, I'm Jack Fisher, the police representative to Harmony House."

Now Amanda understood. Jenna didn't like cops. Too many nasty memories from her bad-girl days.

"I'm Amanda Beeson."

"Are you a friend of Jenna's?"

No, Amanda wanted to shout. But she withheld her instinctive response. "Um, kind of."

"And I presume you didn't come to see me." He smiled as he spoke, which made Amanda relax. But she still had to come up with a reason for being there.

"We, um, came to see a classmate. I guess—I guess

Jenna must have remembered another appointment or something."

"Who are you here to see?"

"Carter Street."

Jack Fisher's forehead puckered. "Carter Street . . . Oh, yes. I don't think he's permitted to have visitors yet."

Amanda pretended that this was news to her. "Oh, that's too bad. How's he doing?"

"I don't really know," the man said apologetically. "I haven't had much to do with him."

Amanda nodded. "Well . . ." No one had come into the area for admission, and she wasn't about to sit around all day for nothing. "I guess I'll go then."

"Hang on a minute. Let me see if I can put you in touch with someone who's working with your friend. What was your name again?"

"Amanda Beeson."

Jack Fisher went over to the receptionist's desk. "Could you check and see if Doctor Paley is available for a moment? One of Carter Street's classmates is here."

The receptionist picked up a phone and made a call. A moment later the police officer returned to Amanda.

"Doctor Paley's coming out to see you. I have

to go now. It was nice to meet you, Amanda."

"Nice to meet you," Amanda echoed. She sank down in a chair and mentally cursed Jenna for getting her into this business. What was she going to say to this Dr. Paley?

A plump, balding man in a white coat came into the reception room. Since Amanda was the only person waiting, he strode toward her with a smile.

"Amanda?"

Amanda forced a smile. "Hello."

"I'm Doctor Paley. Are you from Carter's class?"

Amanda nodded. "How is Carter doing?"

"He's making progress. I can't tell you very much, of course. Do you know what doctor-patient confidentiality means?"

"I'm not sure," Amanda replied.

"It means that everything Carter says or does is just between him and me. Everything's completely private. I can't talk about him, not to you, not to anyone."

Amanda shrugged. "Okay." She wondered why the doctor was telling her this. It wasn't like she was bugging him for information.

"Madame has told me a little about your special class,"

Dr. Paley went on. "You're each quite unique."

Amanda hated talking about the class. She wanted to get out of there. But she couldn't be rude.

"Yes, I guess so."

He smiled. "Don't worry, I'm not going to ask you about your gift. I know it's not easy for any of you, though. Having any kind of special talent can be difficult to live with. I bet sometimes you hate being gifted."

No kidding, Amanda thought. She couldn't help smiling.

"I just want to let you know, Amanda, that I'm always available to talk with you about it. And, of course, anything we discussed would be kept completely private, just between us. I wouldn't even tell Madame, if you didn't want me to."

"Really?"

He nodded. "Call me anytime, or stop by. Okay?"

"Okay," she replied.

He left her, and Amanda went out of the building. The doctor was nice, she thought. And Madame said he could be trusted.

Maybe this adventure hadn't gone according to plan, but she'd come away with something to think about.

Chapter Nine

D R. PALEY MUST HAVE canceled all his other appointments that day. He brought in sandwiches for himself and Paul, and then it was back to the videotape. The doctor left him in the room to watch it alone.

"So you left your home as a gerbil and became a boy again," the doctor was saying. "Why did you decide to switch back to your real shape?"

"I don't know," the boy on the screen replied. "It just happened. One minute I was a gerbil, and then I was a boy."

"Interesting," Dr. Paley murmured. And even though he was off camera and Paul couldn't see him on the screen, he had the feeling the doctor was making notes. "And then what happened?"

"I walked. But I was so hungry . . . I went by a construction site, and some workers were outside eating lunches. There was an open lunch box, and I saw a sandwich inside. No one was looking so I took it. I had a bite, but then this man saw me. And he hit me."

Watching, Paul saw himself flinch, as if he could still feel the blow.

"And then . . . ?" the doctor's voice prompted.

"I ran. He chased me, but he didn't catch me." He paused. "I think maybe I turned into something that could run faster than me. Yeah . . . I was a squirrel for a while. Then I was me again, and I was cold. I saw a store, and there was a coat in the window. I went inside . . ." The boy in the video began to shake.

"What happened?" Dr. Paley asked.

"I tried to take the coat. A man—he started to yell at me. Then he took out a gun. He was going to kill me, just like those men killed my parents. I was really scared. But then I turned into a rat and got away."

"Where did you go next?"

"I found some trash cans. There was food on top of the garbage. I ate some of it. Someone saw me. He threw something at me . . . I think it was a brick. I jumped off the trash can and turned back into myself. There was a grate in the sidewalk behind the trash cans, and it was a little warmer there. I must have fallen asleep. A policeman woke me up."

"Yes, I have the police notes here," Dr. Paley said. "The officer reported that you didn't respond verbally to his questions, but that you obeyed his directions when he told you to get up and come with him. He took you to the police station, where you were given something to eat."

Paul saw a twitch of the lips on his face, almost as if he'd wanted to smile. "A ham sandwich. A bag of potato chips. Two cookies—chocolate chip."

Dr. Paley continued. "The police were unable to identify you. You didn't match any descriptions of missing persons. A representative from social services took you to a youth shelter. Her notes are almost identical to the police officer's notes. You didn't communicate at all, but you followed her directions. At the youth shelter, you were examined by doctors and psychologists. It was determined that you were in some sort of state of shock and that you'd eventually recover. You were then assigned to a foster family—a Mr. and Mrs. Granger, who were already sheltering two foster boys. Is that correct?"

"Yes," Paul said.

"Have you shapeshifted while living with the Grangers?"

"No."

"Why not?"

"I'm not afraid of them. And they might not feed me if I were a rat or a squirrel."

"The Grangers . . . Were they kind to you?"

"Yes."

"They didn't hit you, or yell at you, or threaten you in any way?"

"No."

"But you didn't speak to them, either. Or to the other boys in the house. Why is that, Paul?"

"I couldn't. I was turned off."

As he watched the video, Paul realized that the real Dr. Paley had returned to the room, and he must have heard that last part. He picked up the remote control. "Turned off like this?" he asked, and the screen went blank.

Paul tried to say "yes," but it was too much effort. He simply nodded.

Dr. Paley pulled his chair around to face Paul. "I think

I understand, Paul," he said quietly. "It was easier to just stop—stop *being*. To be a thing instead of a person. Am I right?"

Paul nodded again.

Dr. Paley looked at his watch. "That's enough for now, Paul. Why don't you go out into the garden for a while? I think you could use a little fresh air. Then we'll watch more of the video."

Paul left the office and went downstairs. What the people here called "the garden" wasn't really a garden—at least, there weren't any flowers or plants. It was just a paved outdoor area with a couple of benches and some lawn chairs, and it was surrounded by high wire fences. But the weather was warm, no one else was around, and the lawn chair was more comfortable than the hard chair in Dr. Paley's office. Paul sat back, closed his eyes, and pondered what he'd remembered. He had a lot to think about.

"Hey, get up."

Paul opened his eyes. Three teenage boys, older and bigger than him, had arrived in the garden. Two of them had plopped down in the other two chairs, and the third seemed to want the chair Paul occupied.

"I said, get up!" the boy barked.

Paul did as he was told. He rose from the chair. The boy pushed him aside and sat down.

"Now beat it."

Automatically, Paul turned to leave. But then something inside him made him stop. It was nice out there, the sun was shining, he didn't want to go back to his little room. He didn't want to leave the garden. Why had he just given up his chair so easily? Because the other boy was bigger, and Paul was afraid of him?

"Beat it!" the boy yelled. "Get outta here!"

And a realization hit Paul hard. He didn't have to do what he was told to do. He didn't have to be afraid. Because he had a gift. And now was the time to use it.

He allowed a soft, shivery sensation to engulf him. A moment later a shriek went up from the boys as a huge wolf took over the space where Paul had been standing. The animal opened its mouth, baring large, sharp teeth, and let out a howl. The three boys fled the scene and ran back into the building.

A window flew open. "Omigod!" someone screamed. "Quick, call animal control! There's a wolf in the garden!"

Paul let out another howl, louder this time. It felt wonderful, like a cry of freedom. He ran around the garden, leaping over the chairs and benches. Now more people were looking out the windows and screaming.

"Get the security guard," someone yelled. "He's got a gun!"

Paul froze. He ducked around to the side of the garden, where no one could see him. And he turned back into a boy.

When the security guard appeared, all he saw was a small, thin boy sitting on a lawn chair.

"Did you see a wolf?" the guard asked.

Paul shook his head. Then he got up and went back into the building.

Chapter Ten

I N THE MEADOWBROOK Middle School cafeteria, it was traditional for boys to sit with boys and girls to sit with girls. Even if they were friends, even if they were going together, boys and girls separated at lunch. It wasn't a law, it wasn't school policy—that's just the way it was.

But this was an opportunity to talk to Ken, and Amanda was going to have to break the unwritten rule. So when she picked up her tray she didn't go directly to her usual table, where Nina and her other friends were sitting. She waited until Ken emerged from the line.

"I have to tell you about Harmony House," she said.

He didn't ask why the story couldn't wait for class. His eyes searched the room. "There's a table."

Amanda knew people were looking at them as they

sat down at the empty table together, and she knew that she'd have to answer for this later, but it was unavoidable. She was impressed that Ken didn't even look embarrassed. He really was too cool for words.

"What happened?" he asked. "Did you get inside?"

Amanda shook her head. "There wasn't anyone checking in. But I talked to Doctor Paley."

"About Carter?"

"Not really." She reported the conversation she'd had with the doctor. "I got this feeling he knows all about the kind of gifts we have. And I think he can help us."

"Help us do what?"

She hesitated. She really had no proof of what she was about to say. But she couldn't help herself. It seemed like a possibility, and Ken would be just as interested as she was.

"Help us lose our gifts."

Ken's eyebrows shot up. "You really think so?"

"He's a doctor, Ken. I bet he knows more about our conditions than Madame does."

"Wow," Ken breathed. "Wouldn't that be something . . ." His eyes shifted. "Hi, Nina."

"Hi, Ken. Amanda, Britney's got a big problem. We need you!"

Amanda gritted her teeth. What could she do? Ken might think she was selfish if she didn't rush to the aid of her friend.

"See you in class," Ken said. He picked up his tray and strolled over to a table where some of his friends were sitting. Amanda took her tray back to her usual table, where Britney, Sophie, and Katie were sitting.

Nina hadn't been lying. Poor Britney looked like she was on the verge of tears.

"He hasn't even spoken to me today," she whimpered. "He acts like I'm not even there."

"Who are you talking about?" Amanda asked.

Sophie answered for her. "Tommy Clerk, of course."

Amanda's brow furrowed. "Tommy Clerk?" She looked at the others. "Why is she crying over him?"

Katie frowned at her. "Amanda, where have you been? Britney's been talking about Tommy for weeks!"

Amanda recovered a dim memory of Britney's latest crush. "Oh yeah, right. Sorry, Britney, I forgot."

Real tears began to flow. "How could you forget?"

Britney wailed softly. "I'm in *love* with him!"

It was on the tip of Amanda's tongue to remind her that she'd been in and out of love with half a dozen boys since September, but she managed to keep this to herself. Britney looked up to her, the way Nina used to, and Amanda didn't need any more frenemies. She had to be sympathetic and offer some advice.

"Tell me what happened," she ordered Britney. At the same time, she handed her a tissue.

Britney blew her nose. "He always goes to his locker just before lunch. So I went by there, and I said 'hi.'"

"And then?"

"He said 'hi.'" Fresh tears began to flow. "And that was all! He closed his locker and walked away!"

"Boys can be so cruel," Katie muttered. "Forget about him, Brit. You can do better."

"But I want Tommy!" Britney sobbed. She appealed to Amanda. "What should I do?"

The other girls, even Nina, looked at Amanda and waited expectantly for the Queen Bee to speak. Amanda's status was on the line, and she needed to show them she was still in charge of the clique.

"You're not flirting, that's the problem," she told

Britney firmly. "Saying 'hi' isn't enough. You have to come on a little stronger."

Nina raised her eyebrows. "But you're always saying we should play hard to get. You said boys don't like girls who show how they feel."

Amanda met Nina's doubtful eyes. "Up to a point," she declared. "Tommy might think Britney's out of his league. He could be afraid to speak to her. Boys can be insecure, you know."

Britney gazed at her in amazement. "Really?"

"Absolutely," Amanda said. "You should go over to his table right now. Don't sit down, just ask him something. You've got a class with him, don't you?"

"Biology."

"Okay. Say something about that, ask him something."

"Something like what?"

"It doesn't matter! Just make sure you make eye contact, and when you walk away, look back and give him a little smile. Not too big. Like this." Amanda demonstrated her well-practiced "I'm just a little bit into you" smile.

"And then what?" Britney wanted to know.

"Then it's his turn. Make sure you run into him after the last bell, and I bet he'll ask you if you want to hang out."

"You really think that will work?" Nina asked skeptically.

"Of course it will," Amanda snapped. But even as she spoke, she wasn't really all that sure. Britney had never been able to flirt easily. If she went over to speak to Tommy now, she'd probably start giggling and fumbling with her words. And if Amanda wanted her crew to respect her, she had to show that her advice would result in success for Britney.

There was only one way to guarantee this. As Sophie, Katie, and Nina debated Amanda's proposal, Amanda kept her eyes fixed on Britney. *Poor Britney, so shy, she can be really pathetic when it comes to boys . . .*

That was all it took. In less than a second, Amanda was looking across the table at Other-Amanda. She had taken over Britney's body.

She rose from the table, turned, and searched the cafeteria for Tommy Clerk. She spotted him at a table with some other guys and sauntered over.

She acted as if she was just walking past the

table and then stopped, as if an idea had struck her. "Tommy . . ."

The boy looked up. "Yeah?"

"Do you understand that stuff about plants? What's it called—photo, photo something."

"Photosynthesis?" Tommy asked.

"Yeah, that. Do you know what it is?"

"It's the process when plants turn carbon dioxide and water into carbohydrates and oxygen."

Amanda-Britney had no idea what he was talking about, but this sounded good. "Oh, okay. Thanks!" She turned as if to walk away, and then looked back, aiming her special smile at Tommy. She hoped the smile looked as flirtatious on Britney's face as it did on her own. From the way Tommy's eyes widened, she had a feeling it did.

She sashayed back to her own table, sat down, and fixed her gaze on Other-Amanda. Almost instantly, she found herself back in her own body.

"That was good, Britney!" she exclaimed.

Britney seemed dazed. "Huh?"

"What you just did!"

Britney looked at her blankly. "What did I do?"

"Britney!" Katie exclaimed. "You talked to Tommy!"

"I did?"

Amanda turned to the others and rolled her eyes. "Can you believe her? She must have been so nervous, she blanked out!"

The girls grinned knowingly, and Amanda wasn't surprised when even Britney bought this.

Britney had never been the sharpest crayon in the box.

Chapter Eleven

"YOU TURNED INTO A wolf outside just now, didn't you, Paul?"

Paul nodded.

"Why?"

Paul looked at him helplessly. He wanted to tell Dr. Paley, but the words just wouldn't come.

"Were there other people out in the garden?"

Paul nodded.

"Did they frighten you? Is that why you shapeshifted?" Dr. Paley smiled. "This makes perfect sense, Paul. Many of your fellow students developed their gifts as a response to something uncomfortable."

Paul had mixed feelings about this. He wasn't proud of the fact that he'd been afraid. But he liked being compared to his classmates, knowing he had this in common with them.

"Let's watch some more of your hypnosis video," Dr. Paley said, and he turned on the TV. Paul looked at himself and listened to the off-screen doctor's voice.

"Let's talk about Serena, Paul."

Paul watched his own face contort on the screen. He looked like he was in pain.

"I don't want to talk about her."

Dr. Paley's voice was gentle but firm. "You must, Paul. You betrayed your classmates. It wasn't your fault—she put you under some kind of spell. But you need to face up to what you did. How did you first meet Serena?"

"Mister Jackson brought me to see her."

"Mister Jackson . . . Ah yes, the former principal of your school. Serena hypnotized you and asked you questions. Do you remember this?"

"Yes."

"What did she ask you?"

"She asked me about the gifted class. She asked questions about the students. She asked me what kind of gifts they have."

"And you told her?"

"Yes."

"But Madame had warned the class never to reveal their gifts, isn't that right?"

"Yes." Paul was clearly in great distress. "I didn't want to tell her. I wanted to keep our secret."

"It's all right, Paul," Dr. Paley said. "She probably gave you some kind of posthypnotic suggestion. You couldn't stop yourself. And you were probably afraid of those people. For good reason, too. They were dangerous people. You have nothing to be ashamed about, Paul. Your classmates will forgive you."

The boy on the screen seemed to relax a little.

Dr. Paley hit the pause button and turned to Paul. "There's one thing that puzzles me, though, Paul. We were talking about your shapeshifting ability as a response to fear. If you were afraid of Serena, Mister Jackson, and the other people in that group, why didn't you shift? You could have become some kind of large animal. You could have attacked them. Or you could have become a small animal and escaped. Why didn't that happen, Paul? Why didn't you shift?"

Again, Paul could only look at him helplessly. This time, the doctor had no speculations to offer. "You're not sure. You probably don't even remember. Well, let's get back to the video."

But Paul knew perfectly well why he hadn't shifted when he was with those bad people. He didn't know then that he *could*. It was true that he'd shifted before, at home, when the bad guys shot his parents. But back when he was turned off, he didn't know he could do it on purpose—he didn't know that he had some control over this strange and mysterious gift.

But he knew now.

Chapter Twelve

N THE GIFTED CLASS, Ken ran in at the last minute so Amanda didn't get a chance to talk to him before Madame called for everyone's attention.

But before Madame had even said "good afternoon," Ken's hand shot up. Madame looked at him in surprise.

"Yes, Ken?"

"Madame, could I ask the class something? There's something I've been thinking about a lot lately."

"Of course, Ken. What's on your mind?"

His classmates turned to look at him.

Ken was clearly uncomfortable at being the center of attention, but he persevered. "I want to know . . . If you could get rid of your gift, would you? I mean, most of you guys know how I don't like hearing these voices. And I was just wondering if I was the only one who doesn't like having a gift."

"It's not always comfortable having a gift, Ken," Madame said.

"Yeah, yeah, I know that," Ken interrupted. "I'm sorry, Madame, but I'm not talking about getting used to the gift. I want to know if anyone else wants to get rid of their gift."

An uncomfortable silence fell over the room. Amanda hastened to break it. "I'd like to get rid of my gift. I know there's no way I can," she added hastily, "but if I could, I would."

"Sometimes I wish I didn't have my gift," Emily offered. "When I get these images of terrible things about to happen . . ." She shuddered.

"You just have to learn to control it," Jenna declared, "so you don't see the future unless you want to. That's what I do. I mean, if I had to hear everyone's thoughts all the time, I'd go crazy. But I'm okay with it now."

Tracey agreed. "It's like Madame says—we need to figure out ways to use our gifts well."

"That's right," Madame said.

"No," came a quiet voice from the back.

Everyone turned to look at Sarah.

"I'd give anything to lose my gift," Sarah said.

Amanda thought Madame looked very upset. The teacher's lips tightened, and she folded her arms across her chest. She seemed to be gathering her thoughts and choosing her next words carefully.

"Class . . . I want you to listen to me. I know there are many times when your gifts may seem like burdens— or curses, even. But they're not, you know. Each one of your gifts is a blessing."

"Yeah, that's what I think," Charles said. "It makes my life a lot easier."

"It's not just that, Charles," Madame continued. "You were given these gifts for a reason, and we don't really know what that reason is. But they're not to be wished away! They have a purpose, and our goal is to discover the purpose. You're here to learn, not to give up."

"It's not like you have a choice, anyway," Martin commented. "You can't lose your gift."

"But if we *could*—" Ken began.

"No!" Madame interrupted, and Amanda was startled by the tone of her voice. This was unusual. She always let the students have their say. And her voice was almost shrill. "You can't! It would be like losing your heart— your brain. This gift is part of who you are. You must cherish it, even if you can't understand it! Ken, I know you care about people, and with your gift you can help them. Amanda . . ." She practically glared at her. "Amanda, if you could stop thinking about your gift as a personal inconvenience, maybe you could help people, too!"

Amanda couldn't remember ever hearing Madame sound so emotional. It was weird. And how dare she pick on Amanda like that! Strong, conflicting emotions filled her, and she didn't know which was stronger—her pity for Madame's distress or her anger at being singled out.

Pity must have been the stronger one, because suddenly she was looking at the class through Madame's eyes.

"Madame, are you okay?" Jenna asked.

Quickly, Amanda blocked her thoughts so Jenna couldn't read them. Not that Jenna would even try—Madame was an expert at blocking Jenna.

"I'm fine," she said. She glanced at Other-Amanda, who had taken out her makeup bag and was now examining her face in a mirror. Sometimes she wondered why others were so easily fooled by the robot version of herself. She wasn't *that* vain.

The whole class was watching her expectantly.

Amanda-Madame pulled her shoulders back, held her head high, and hoped she was doing a good imitation of Madame's erect posture. It was time to have some fun!

"Now, class, we're going to test the level of control we have over our gifts. We will begin with Tracey. Tracey, make yourself invisible right now."

"Um, I can *try*," Tracey said. "It doesn't always work."

"Just do it!" Amanda-Madame snapped.

Tracey didn't seem very happy about the order, but she obediently closed her eyes and scrunched up her face, as if she was concentrating very hard. Seconds later, she vanished.

"Very good," Amanda-Madame pronounced. "Now come back."

Nothing happened.

Jenna spoke. "She doesn't have as much control coming back as she has disappearing."

"Obviously," Amanda-Madame said. "Emily . . . Look into the future and tell us when Tracey will reappear."

Emily stared at Tracey's empty desk for a moment. "Tracey will be back before the bell rings," she predicted.

"All right." The fake teacher turned to Charles. "Charles, we know you can make things move. I want to know how precise your gift is. Please move my desk six inches to the left."

Charles looked at the desk and shrugged. "Sure." The heavy wooden desk rose slightly and moved to the left.

"Does anyone have a ruler or measuring tape?" Amanda-Madame asked.

"I think there's a measuring tape in your top drawer," Emily said.

For a second, Amanda-Madame was confused and looked at the desk in which the robot was sitting. She recovered quickly. "Yes, of course, that's right." She went into the drawer of the teacher's desk and took out a measuring tape.

"Hmm . . . You seem to have only moved the desk four inches, Charles. You must improve."

"Two inches, big deal," Charles protested.

"Charles! We aim for perfection here!"

Charles shrank back in his wheelchair. "Yes, Madame," he murmured.

It was getting very hard for Amanda not to burst out laughing. This was fun!

"Yes, Madame."

At least the teacher didn't go on and on about it. She gave them a reading assignment, the bell rang, and she dismissed them.

Amanda turned to Ken. "We have to talk," she said urgently. She glanced at the door, which someone had already opened. Nina wasn't there—not yet, at least. "And we have to talk *alone*."

Ken got the message. He got up and followed Amanda out. She led him down the corridor and into the first empty classroom they came to.

She knew there was a custodian who came around to make sure rooms were empty, so she didn't waste any time, even if it meant coming off as a little pushy.

"I don't care what Madame says," she declared flatly. "If someone like this Doctor Paley can get rid of our gifts, I'm totally up for it."

"Me, too," Ken agreed. "Though I have to say that was pretty funny, what you pulled back in class."

"I guess it was kind of mean, what I did to Sarah," she confessed.

"Not really," Ken said thoughtfully. "She needed a push. She has big problems dealing with her gift. She has to confront it sooner or later. I think you did her a good deed."

Amanda preened. "I just thought I'd have one last crazy fling before giving up this gift for good. Do you want a long last talk with any ghosts?"

Ken's smile faded.

"What's the matter?"

"I'm thinking about Jack."

"Oh." She knew who Ken was referring to. Jack Farrell had been Ken's best buddy, and he'd died in that accident on the field. His was the first voice from beyond the grave that Ken had heard. "You still talk to him?"

"Not that much," Ken admitted. "Not like before. I guess he's comfortable now, wherever he is. He doesn't need me like he used to."

"So if you lost your gift and Jack couldn't reach you anymore, that would be okay?"

"Yeah, I guess so."

She wished he sounded more sure of himself. "Just think about it, Ken. No more ghosts asking you to check on their grandsons or watch soap operas."

"And no more gifted class," Ken added.

"Exactly. We could be normal, Ken. Wouldn't that be nice?"

He looked at her and smiled. "Yeah. Really nice. But we don't know for sure if Doctor Paley can do this."

"No, not for sure," Amanda admitted. "But we can try. I feel like this is right for us. Don't you?"

"Yeah." Then he fell silent, but Amanda didn't mind at all, because he was looking deeply into her eyes.

The custodian came in. "Out," he said.

They left the room—and ran right into Britney.

"There you are!" Britney exclaimed. "Nina was looking for you. And so was I. Guess what? It worked!"

Amanda looked at her blankly. "What worked?"

"What you made me do at lunch. Tommy just asked me to meet him at the mall! It happened, just like you said it would."

"Great," Amanda replied.

"It's funny, though," Britney went on. "I still can't remember actually talking to him in the cafeteria."

"You were nervous," Amanda told her.

Britney grinned. "I guess. But I'm not nervous now! I gotta go and meet Tommy. I'll call you tonight and tell you what happened."

She took off, and Ken turned to Amanda. "You did it, didn't you? You took over her body and came on to Tommy."

Amanda lowered her eyes modestly. "I kind of had to. She'd never do it on her own."

Ken smiled. "That was nice of you."

She loved the way he was looking at her. It occurred to her that she had a connection with him that Nina could never have. And when they lost their gifts together . . . it would link them in a way that could last forever.

Chapter Thirteen

PAUL CARTER WAS DREAMING, but not about a boy or a TV. He was dreaming about animals. He dreamed about an elephant, a tiger, a monkey. And they were all him.

He was hanging from the limb of a tree and swinging his legs. He leaped from branch to branch, and he could actually feel the motion. But then bad men approached, and they were carrying guns.

So he dropped from the tree and became an elephant. With his trunk, he swept the men off the ground and flung them far, far away. And then he became a cat, a soft, fuzzy cat, curled on someone's lap, being petted . . . That felt really nice. And then he was a lion, running for the pure pleasure of running, happy and unafraid. Who could hurt the king of the jungle?

When he woke up on Thursday morning, something struck him. For the first time in a long, long time, he didn't feel frightened. And he didn't go immediately into his morning routine of watering the plant, brushing his teeth, getting dressed. He stayed in his bed and had some wide-awake dreams.

He pictured himself back at Meadowbrook Middle School, in his gifted class. Charles talked about moving things with his mind. Jenna reported on what someone else was thinking. Emily predicted something that was going to happen.

And Carter—no, *Paul* Carter—told them how he'd been a bird that morning. How he'd flown to school. How he was planning to fly to Mexico . . .

What would it be like, to actually have a story to tell? All these months, he'd listened to tales of the others' gifts. He always felt like an outsider, like he wasn't supposed to be there. He'd been stuck in the class only because nobody knew what to do with him.

But now he could belong in the class. He could be part of the group. He was gifted, too.

Suddenly, he wanted to test his gift. He got out of bed and considered the possibilities. The first image that came to mind was the pet he always wanted.

He could feel it, the changes in his body, but it

didn't hurt at all. And now he was a dog, a big dog. A German shepherd. He leaped back up on the bed so he could see himself in the mirror over the sink. He was beautiful! And in joy, he opened his mouth and let out a howl.

Immediately, there was a pounding on his door. "What's going on in there? Open this door!"

Paul shifted back. He went to the door and opened it. An angry resident assistant stood outside.

"Do you have a dog in here?"

Paul shook his head.

The guy looked at him suspiciously and pushed him aside. *I could become a snake and bite him*, Paul thought. He didn't—but it was nice knowing he could.

The resident assistant went to Paul's closet and looked inside. Then he bent down and checked under the bed. Finally he gave up, and with one last dark look at Paul, he left.

Paul suddenly realized that his face felt funny, like it was twitching or something. He went to the mirror, looked at his reflection, and realized why. He was smiling.

A glance at the clock on the wall told him he was late.

Quickly, he watered the plant, washed his face, and got dressed.

At breakfast, he didn't join in any conversations, but he found himself listening and paying more attention to the others at his table. One of the older boys was bragging about the act that had sent him to Harmony House.

"So this lady is holding her purse really tightly, and I figure there's gotta be a reason. She's carrying something valuable. So I come up from behind and tap her on the shoulder. "Excuse me," I say, real polite and smiling, "could you tell me where the First National Bank is?" She starts to think, and I grab the purse and take off. She's like so freaked out, I'm halfway around the corner before she even starts yelling!"

Paul imagined himself on the street and watching the event occur. What would he have done? If the thief was a fast runner, Paul could have become a cheetah. Wasn't that the fastest animal? Or he could shift into a tiger, pounce on the thief, take the purse in his teeth, and bring it back to the lady.

He felt himself smiling again. It was exciting, think-ing about all the possibilities. He noticed that people at the table were looking at him oddly. Had he shifted without even trying? No, he decided, it was probably because they'd never seen him smile before.

He was still smiling when he arrived at Dr. Paley's office. Dr. Paley smiled back at him.

"I can see you're feeling well, Paul. But if I ask, 'How are you?' would you be able to answer me?"

It took a lot of effort and a few false tries, but finally Paul managed to murmur something that sounded pretty close to "fine."

Dr. Paley nodded with approval. "It's going to take a while before you'll be able to speak normally when fully conscious. You'll have to practice. I'm going to see if I can arrange for a speech therapist to work with you."

Paul was pleased. He wanted to be able to speak easily. When he was allowed to go back to school, he wanted to tell his classmates how he'd turned into a dog that morning and alarmed the resident assistant. He remembered Charles telling a funny story once, about how he teased his brother by moving his chair just as he was about to sit down. People laughed . . .

Madame had scolded him, though. She'd said Charles shouldn't use his gift for silly reasons. Paul would have to start seriously listening to what Madame said now.

But maybe it was okay, just once in a while, to do something silly with a gift . . .

"Are you thinking about your gift?" Dr. Paley asked.

Paul nodded.

"It must be pretty shocking to suddenly realize how much power you have," the doctor said.

Paul nodded again, though *shocking* didn't seem to be the right word to describe his reaction. Maybe at first, when he saw himself as a rabbit on the TV screen. Now he was more . . . *interested*.

"These kinds of gifts . . . They can be frightening," the doctor continued. "You must have heard your classmates talk about that."

Paul thought back to the discussions in the gifted class. Yes, some people talked about being scared. Amanda worried that she might get stuck in the body of someone she'd taken over. Sarah . . . She was definitely scared, she wouldn't even talk about her gift.

"You know, with your gift you could become very dangerous."

Paul could see how that could happen. Animals can hurt people. Of course *people* could hurt people, too. But if you were a good person—or a good animal—you wouldn't do that. Madame talked a lot about controlling the gifts . . . He'd have to pay attention to her so he could learn how to use his gift well.

"Madame believes that most of your classmates developed their gifts as a reaction to something. Or perhaps as a compensation. They developed these gifts because they needed them to survive. Martin was small and weak. People teased him, and he dealt with this by becoming unnaturally strong. Charles felt trapped in his wheelchair and unable to do things on his own. So his mind became so strong that he could move objects with it. As for you . . ."

The doctor leaned back in his chair and studied Paul.

"Your gift emerged through fear. Are you still afraid, Paul?"

Paul worked at forming the word, and he was pleased that it came out almost clearly. "No."

"Good!" Dr. Paley said. "Then perhaps you don't really need your gift. The goal, Paul, is to become normal. For example, Madame tells me that Martin has been growing, and he's just about reached a normal height and weight. I believe that when his subconscious accepts the fact that he doesn't need superstrength to fight his battles, he may naturally lose his gift."

That made sense to Paul.

"Madame told me about . . ." he studied some papers on his desk. ". . . Emily. She predicts the future, right? And do you know when she discovered this gift?"

The word that came from Paul's mouth sounded like "fahzer," but Dr. Paley understood.

"That's right. Her father was killed in an accident, and Emily claims to have seen it in her head before it happened. But my theory is that Emily subconsciously created that memory after the fact. And this triggered an actual ability to predict the future." He gazed up at the ceiling. "Is this a good thing? I don't think so. It could have grave consequences if Emily's visions become clearer and more accurate. This could change the course of history. Emily doesn't need this gift. I don't think any of you really need your gifts."

Paul didn't agree. He got some words out. "Charles . . . chair." They sounded like "Shar" and "sheer," but Dr. Paley got the picture.

"You're saying Charles needs his gift because it's not

likely that he'll ever be out of a wheelchair. But most people in wheelchairs don't have supernatural gifts, Paul, and they function perfectly well." He smiled. "Now, I don't know Charles personally, but I wonder if perhaps his gift emerged simply because he's too lazy to learn how to do things on his own. I do believe you'd all survive very well without your gifts. You'd probably be happier."

Paul wasn't so sure about that. *Happy* . . . It wasn't a word he normally associated with himself. But since discovering his gift, he might be tempted to call himself happy.

Dr. Paley looked at his watch. "That will be all for today, Paul." He rose and opened the door. Halfway out, Paul remembered something he wanted to ask the doctor. When would he be able to leave Harmony House? But before he could formulate words, the phone on the secretary's desk rang.

"Doctor Paley's office. Yes, send them in." She hung up the phone. "Ken Preston and Amanda Beeson have arrived for their appointment."

"Good," Dr. Paley said. "I'll see you tomorrow, Paul."

But Paul was curious. Why were two of his class-mates coming to see Dr. Paley? Did it have something to do with what the doctor was just talking to him about?

Before, Paul wouldn't have cared about Ken and Amanda. But now that he was one of them . . .

The secretary had her back to him. Paul shifted. And fortunately, Dr. Paley was studying his notes—so he didn't notice the cockroach that crawled under his desk.

CHAPTER FOURTEEN

THE SECRETARY TOLD KEN and Amanda that Dr. Paley was expecting them. Sure enough, when they entered the inner office, the plump, balding man in the white coat was standing by his desk and smiling.

"Come in, Amanda. And you must be Ken. Have a seat."

Amanda surveyed the room, and what she saw was reassuring. It looked like any doctor's office, with an examining table, a cabinet holding medical equipment, and a tall weighing scale. It was all spotlessly clean, even the floor, so she felt okay about dropping her purse there when she sat down.

"So, are you kids cutting class?" the doctor asked jovially.

"We have excuses," Amanda assured him. She didn't want him thinking she and Ken were the kind of people who were residents of Harmony House. "I told the school secretary we had doctors' appointments."

"Which is absolutely true," Dr. Paley said. He indicated a framed diploma on the wall behind his desk. "I *am* a doctor."

Amanda had no doubts about that. If Madame trusted this man, he had to be what he said he was. Madame was no fool.

"Now, tell me what I can do for you."

Amanda looked at Ken.

"You go first," Ken said.

She faced the doctor. "When I saw you yesterday, you said you might be able to help us. And . . . and we need help.

"Help with what?" Dr. Paley asked.

Amanda glanced at Ken again. Ken nodded, clearly encouraging her to go on.

"Help us to get rid of these gifts."

"Ah." The doctor opened a folder and turned some pages. "Now, let me see. Amanda, you're suffering from psycho-transitional corporeality—you're a 'body snatcher,' is that correct?"

Amanda grimaced. "That makes me sound like a criminal."

Dr. Paley smiled. "It's just the term that's used for what you're capable of doing. You can inhabit the consciousness of others."

"It started when I was a little kid. I saw a woman begging on a street, and I felt sorry for her. And then, suddenly, I *was* her."

"You didn't *try* to become her?"

"No! Who wants to be some poor, dirty beggar? It just happened, I couldn't do anything about it. I was looking through her eyes. I could even see myself, staring at her. Me. Whatever."

Dr. Paley regarded her thoughtfully. "You were in two places at once?"

"Not exactly," Amanda told him. "It wasn't like I could feel myself being me. But the girl . . . She acted like me, she talked like me. She wasn't like, *dead*, or a zombie. Every time this happens to me, when I can see myself, I'm acting like me. Does that make sense?" She looked at Ken for support.

"It's sort of like she has a clone," Ken offered. "Or she's a robot that's been programmed to be her."

"I see," Dr. Paley said, making some notes. "And you say this has happened other times?"

Amanda nodded. She described the time she became Tracey, back when Tracey was a major nerd and loser. She told him about the young woman she'd met at a séance, who was depressed because her mother had died. She didn't mention the time she'd become Ken. They never talked about that—it was just too creepy.

"And this happens because you feel sorry for the people. Can you stop it from happening?"

"Sometimes," Amanda said. "If I try really hard, I can think of them as absurd instead of pitiful."

Dr. Paley understood. "You treat them with scorn instead of pity."

"I guess. Sort of. Just so I don't, you know, body-snatch."

Ken jumped in. "That's how she got her reputation. Some kids call her the Queen of Mean."

Amanda was taken aback. "Where did you hear that?" she asked him.

"Nina told me."

Amanda gritted her teeth. That figured.

"Does this ever happen if you *want* to be someone else?" Dr. Paley asked.

"No, I like being me. Why would I want to be someone pitiful?" And then she realized she had an opportunity to salvage her reputation for Ken's sake. "Actually, I did do it on purpose recently. To save someone."

"What happened?" Ken and the doctor asked simultaneously.

Amanda preened. It was cool, having all this attention and a story to tell that would make her look like a really nice person.

She told the story of the hitchhiker. Ken was totally blown away.

"Wow! You might have saved that girl's life!"

Amanda smiled modestly. "Yes, that's what Jenna said."

But Dr. Paley didn't look very impressed. "And you might have found yourself being abducted in the hitch-hiker's place."

Amanda stopped smiling. "I didn't think of that," she admitted.

"Your gift has dangerous implications," Dr. Paley

noted. "Ken, what about your gift? How do you feel about it?"

"It's mainly annoying," Ken said. He explained to the doctor how it all began, when he collided with his best friend Jack on the playing field. "It wasn't so bad when it was just Jack contacting me. But then I started hearing from all these other dead people. Some of them just wanted to talk, but a lot of them asked me to do favors for them."

"And did you do these favors?"

"Once in a while," Ken said. "Like, I've been watching a soap opera so I can tell this old lady what's happening on it. But sometimes, people want me to get involved in their lives. This one guy, he wanted me to contact his granddaughter and tell her that her boyfriend was no good. I said no." He paused. "I kind of felt bad about it, though."

"So your gift doesn't bring you any pleasure," Dr. Paley commented.

Ken shook his head. Amanda noticed he didn't mention the time he was able to save a young boy's impoverished family by talking to the boy's late father and finding out where the man had left a winning lottery ticket. She couldn't blame him for not telling the doctor. One decent experience didn't make up for a zillion obnoxious ones.

"Your gift could be dangerous, too," Dr. Paley told Ken.

"How?" Ken asked.

"You might feel very sympathetic to someone's plight and get involved in something that could harm you."

Ken considered this. "Yeah, I guess that could happen."

Dr. Paley gazed at them both seriously. "I can see that your gifts cause both of you a lot of problems. And I agree, your lives would be easier without them."

"Is it possible?" Amanda asked. "Is there any way we can get rid of our gifts?"

"It's . . . possible," Dr. Paley said slowly. "There's research going on now, and there are indications that a type of brain surgery could erase this kind of ability."

Amanda made a face. "Brain surgery? That sounds pretty scary."

"Actually, it's not as dramatic as it sounds," the doctor told her. "It's a totally noninvasive procedure."

"What does that mean?" Ken asked.

"Special scans identify the brain element that's responsible for the gift. The area is treated with a laser beam. No cuts or incisions are made. The patient wouldn't even need an anaesthetic."

Amanda still didn't feel comfortable with the idea. "Would they have to shave your head?"

Dr. Paley smiled. "No, that wouldn't be necessary."

"Does it cost a lot?" Ken wanted to know.

"Actually, it's all experimental at this point. The patients who have received the treatments were all volunteers, part of a research study. So there was no charge." After a moment, he added, "I'm a member of this research team."

Amanda drew in her breath. "So does that mean you could do this laser thing to us?"

"I would have to consult with the other members of the team, of course. But, yes, it is possible that the procedure could take place right here in this office."

Amanda didn't know what to say. Ken was speechless, too.

"Now, as I said, this is all experimental," Dr. Paley went on. "There are no guarantees. But no one has been injured by the procedure yet."

The word *yet* hung in the air. Amanda tried to ignore it.

"How come Madame never told us about this?" Ken wanted to know.

"Madame doesn't know about it," the doctor said. "Very few people do. Let me ask you something. Do you tell many people about your gift?"

"No, of course not," Ken said. "No one would believe it."

"And if they did," Amanda added, "they'd think we were weird."

"Exactly," Dr. Paley said. "Most people don't believe that these abilities exist. And most people aren't intellectually or emotionally capable of dealing with such knowledge. Therefore, procedures to correct the problem have also been kept highly confidential. And that's why you must not tell anyone about this procedure."

"Not even Madame?" Ken asked.

Amanda answered before Dr. Paley could. "Especially not Madame. She'd try to talk us out of it. Remember, she told us we've been blessed."

"Madame is a very fine person," Dr. Paley said, "but

she is not gifted. No matter how much she cares for you all, she can't really understand you."

Amanda thought of another reason. "And don't forget, if there weren't any so-called gifted students to teach, she wouldn't have a job."

"Are there other students in your class who'd be interested in losing their gifts?" Dr. Paley asked.

Ken and Amanda looked at each other. "Sarah," they said in unison.

Dr. Paley looked at his notes and frowned. "Sarah . . . I don't think Madame has mentioned her."

"She's got the most powerful gift of all," Ken told him. "She can make anyone do anything."

"But she never does," Amanda said. "Well, maybe once or twice. She stopped a man from getting his hands on a gun. But I've never seen her do anything really big."

"Interesting," Dr. Paley murmured. He made a note. "Well, I give you permission to tell Sarah about the procedure. And if she's interested, you can bring her along on Friday."

"Friday," Ken repeated. "You mean—tomorrow?"

Dr. Paley nodded. "I'm going to talk to my colleagues today, and if all goes well, we should be able to perform the procedure tomorrow. Leave me your cell phone numbers and I'll send you text messages later."

Amanda was stunned. She had no idea everything could happen this fast. "Don't we need to get our parents' permission?"

"Do your parents know about your gifts?" Dr. Paley asked.

Amanda and Ken both shook their heads.

"Do you want to tell them about your gifts?"

They looked at each other, and then both of them shook their heads again.

"Well, then . . ."

They gave the doctor their phone numbers. Amanda picked up her purse, and they left the office. Walking back through the building, she still felt like she was in a state of shock. Ken finally broke the silence.

"Wow."

And Amanda responded: "Yeah."

They entered the reception area, but before they could reach the door, a voice called out. "Well, hello again!"

Amanda turned. That good-looking police officer from the day before, Jack Something, approached her with a smile. Somehow, even though she was feeling dazed, she managed to smile back.

"Hello. This is my friend, Ken."

"Hi, Ken, I'm Jack Fisher. What are you guys doing here?"

Amanda thought rapidly. "Um, I thought maybe I could try again. You know, to see Carter. We have to get back to school now." She tugged at Ken's arm.

"You're at Meadowbrook Middle, right? I'm going in that direction, I'll give you a lift."

They walked outside together. "Hey, this is cool," Ken said. "I hope people see us getting out of a police car at school."

Jack started the car. "Your friends will think you guys are the new Bonnie and Clyde."

"Who?" Amanda asked.

"They were a couple of bank robbers in the 1930s," Jack told her.

"Oh. I wasn't born then."

Jack laughed. "Neither was I." Just then, there was a loud buzzing sound, and a voice came out over the car radio.

"All cars in the vicinity of Dover and Crane, proceed to incident in the five-hundred block. I repeat . . ."

Immediately, Jack made a U-turn and took off at high speed. The intersection of Dover and Crane was less than a minute away. When they reached the scene, just outside a tall office building, they saw an ambulance. Another cop came over to the car, and Jack rolled down the window.

"What's going on?" he asked.

"Suicide," the other cop said. "Guy who was just fired from his job jumped from the top of the building."

"Oh, that's bad," Jack murmured.

"Gets worse," the cop said. "He left a note. It says he left a bomb in the building and it's set to go off in fifteen minutes. We're trying to evacuate all the buildings on the street, but I don't know if we can get everyone out in time. And we have no idea where in the building the bomb is located." His face was grim. "Fifteen stories, Jack."

Jack jumped out of the car and opened the back door. "Sorry, you two, I won't be able to give you a lift. And I need you to leave the area immediately."

Amanda didn't need any encouragement. She climbed out of the back seat, and Ken followed her. More police cars were arriving, and they hurried to get out of the way.

"Omigod, I can't believe this," Amanda exclaimed.

"There have to be hundreds of people in all those buildings. Maybe thousands! This is terrible!"

When Ken didn't respond, she turned to look at him. He'd stopped running, and he was several yards behind her. "Ken! Hurry up!"

"Wait," he said.

"Are you crazy?" she shrieked. "Wait for what? For the bomb to go off?"

Ken held up his hand, like he was telling her to stop talking. She knew the expression on his face. One of his dead correspondents had just checked in.

"Ken, tell the soap opera lady you'll call her back!" she wailed.

"Okay," Ken whispered. But Amanda didn't think he was speaking to *her*. Then he blinked.

"Amanda, I have to find Jack. You go on without me."

How many shocks could a girl take in one day? Amanda watched Ken move in the direction of the building. People were pouring out of it now, and there was panic in the air. She knew she should get as far away as she could, as fast as she could. But she just stood there, watching Ken walk closer and closer to the danger. And then she ran after him.

When she caught up with him, he'd just spotted Jack. The police officer saw him, and he looked angry. "What are you kids doing? I told you to get out of here!"

"I know where the bomb is," Ken said.

Jack stared at him. "What?"

"I know where the bomb is. It's in the men's bathroom on the tenth floor."

Jack's eyes narrowed. "How could you possibly know this?"

"I can't—I can't explain it now. There's still time—you can find the bomb and dismantle it. It's a simple timing device. You just have to switch it off."

Jack frowned. "Look, if you're playing some kind of game—"

"I'm not, I'm telling the truth, you gotta believe me!" Ken pleaded.

Jack grabbed the arm of another cop passing by. "Put these two in a car," he ordered. And he took off.

The cop grabbed Ken's arm with one hand and Amanda's arm with the other.

"Hey, that hurts!" Amanda cried in outrage.

The cop ignored her. He opened the back door of a police car and pushed them both in. Then he slammed the door. Amanda had seen enough police shows on TV to know they wouldn't be able to get out on their own.

She was pretty sure she knew what had just happened. She turned to Ken. "Did the suicide guy contact you?"

He nodded. "He was really upset about losing his job, but it wasn't just that. He was having a rough time in lots of ways. And he was angry at all his coworkers for something—I don't know what. So he planted the bomb and then he jumped out the window. But now he feels bad about it. He doesn't really want to hurt anyone."

Ken sank back in his seat and started rubbing his forehead. Instinctively, Amanda reached out and took his other hand. Maybe she was being pushy, but for once she didn't care. This felt like the right thing to do.

They sat there together in silence. From the window, Amanda could see a couple of guys in what looked like space suits go into the building. She didn't know how much more time passed—it felt like an eternity, but when she looked at her watch, she realized it had only been 20 minutes since they left Dr. Paley's office.

Suddenly, the back door of their car opened. A very

weary-looking Jack Fisher stood there. "Okay, you can get out."

"Did you find the bomb?" Ken asked.

"Yes. It's been dismantled."

Ken let out his breath. "Okay."

Jack's eyes bore into him. "What I need to find out now is how you knew where the bomb was."

Ken scratched the side of his head. "It's—it's kind of hard to explain."

"You're coming to headquarters with me," Jack said flatly. "You can explain it to me there." He turned to Amanda. "You go back to school. I'll have someone take you."

"Can't I stay with Ken?" she asked.

Ken shot her an appreciative look. "You go on," he said. "Tell Madame what happened."

Jack beckoned to another cop and told him to take Amanda to Meadowbrook Middle School. She'd turned to go off with him when Ken called to her.

"Amanda . . . just tell Madame what happened *here*. You know what I mean."

She did. She had no intention of telling Madame what they'd discussed with Dr. Paley.

Chapter Fifteen

COCKROACHES MUST *have excellent hearing ability*, Paul thought. Despite the fact that he was encased in leather and practically buried under a lot of stuff, he'd understood everything that went on outside Amanda's purse.

It had been easy for Paul to get into Amanda's purse. She'd put it on the floor next to her chair in Dr. Paley's office, and it had a drawstring fastening. Paul didn't have any problem crawling in, and no one saw him. But now he had to make a fast decision: should he remain in Amanda's purse, wedged between her makeup bag and her wallet, or figure out a way to leave with Ken?

Amanda would be going back to school, and Paul was tempted to go along with her. He missed Madame, he wanted to see his classmates, to find out what they'd been up to—and to hear what they might say about him. Had they forgiven him, like Dr. Paley said they would?

On the other hand, Ken was heading for police head-quarters, where he'd be questioned about the bomb. And that could be very exciting.

Who should he choose? Who was more interesting? He could feel the bag moving. Amanda was about to get out of the police car. He quickly climbed out of her bag and dropped out. Then he scrambled across the back seat and climbed into the pocket of Ken's jacket. Luckily, everyone was too distracted by what was going on to see the bug make his journey.

In the darkness of the pocket, Paul couldn't see anything, but he heard Jack the cop return to the car and start up the engine. There wasn't much else to hear, though. Jack didn't say anything, and Ken was silent, too. He was probably trying to come up with a way to explain how he knew about the bomb.

Paul recalled all those times in class when Ken said he thought his gift was worthless. He'd told Dr. Paley that he didn't get any pleasure from his gift. But he'd just saved the lives of a lot of people. *Surely he must be feeling something*, Paul thought.

He heard the car stop and the doors opening, and

he felt Ken move. Then he heard the buzz of many conversations, phones ringing, people moving around. They must be in the police headquarters.

"We'll go into my office," Jack said.

He heard a door close, and then it was quiet.

"Sit down, Ken," the police officer said. "Now, tell me what happened back there."

"I didn't have anything to do with that bomb," Ken said.

"But you knew where it was," Jack declared.

"Yes. Well, no. I mean, I just sort of guessed."

"That's not true, Ken. You were very precise about the location."

Ken said nothing. Paul heard the rustle of papers, and then Jack spoke again.

"Did you know this Mister Patterson? Arnold Patterson?"

"Is that the man who jumped out of the building?" Ken asked.

"Yes. Isn't the name familiar to you?"

"No."

"You don't know him?"

"No. Well, not exactly."

"Explain what you mean, Ken." The police officer's tone wasn't harsh, but it was clear that he was determined to get an answer.

For a few seconds, Ken was silent. Then he let out a long sigh. "I never actually met him. But . . . he spoke to me."

"When?"

"Today."

"He called you on the phone before he jumped out of the building?"

"No. Not on the phone. And not before he jumped."

Now Jack sounded exasperated. "Ken, you're not making any sense."

"I heard him. *After* he jumped."

"I don't understand. You weren't anywhere near Patterson. And according to the investigator, he died on impact. He couldn't have spoken to you after he jumped."

"He did," Ken said stubbornly.

"Ken, tell me the truth!"

"What's the point?" Ken cried out. "You won't believe me."

"Try me," Jack said quietly.

There was a pause, and then Ken spoke in a dull, flat voice. "I hear dead people."

"What?"

"Dead people talk to me."

There was another pause. "I think you can come up with a better story than that, Ken."

"It's true, I swear it!"

"How does that happen, Ken?"

"I'm not sure. I just hear them, in my head."

"So . . . this wasn't the first time?"

"It started in September," Ken said. "I was on the soccer field, and I ran into my best friend. His name was Jack, too. Jack Farrell."

"Go on."

"We were both knocked out. I recovered. Jack died."

The pocket where Paul was resting must have been close to Jack's heart. He could hear it beating faster.

"After he died, Jack started talking to me."

"What did he say?"

"He said he didn't blame me for the accident. He asked me to look out for his girlfriend. He still talks to me once in a while. Mostly, he just wants to know what's happening at school, what his pals are up to, that kind of thing. But then other dead people started talking to me, too."

"What do they say to you?"

"Sometimes they ask me for a favor. Mostly, they just want to talk."

"I see," Jack said.

"You think I'm nuts, don't you?" Ken asked. "I'm not. But I don't like hearing these voices. That's what I was talking to Doctor Paley about at Harmony House. He might be able to help me."

"So this is what that gifted class is all about," Jack remarked.

"You know about the class?"

"I knew Jenna was in it, and I suspected there was something unusual about her. What about your friend Amanda? Does she have a gift, too?"

"I'm not supposed to talk about it," Ken said.

"That's okay, you don't have to tell me what their gifts are," Jack told him. "Everything's starting to make sense now. This Patterson guy, he had regrets about leaving the bomb behind, so he told you where it could be found."

"Exactly," Ken said. "You really believe me? You understand?"

"I won't say I understand," Jack said carefully, "but there's a lot in this world that can't be explained. I try to keep an open mind. Yes, I believe you, Ken. That's quite a gift you have."

"I don't like it," Ken blurted out. "It's creepy. Doctor Paley says maybe he can help me lose it."

"Well, it was certainly useful in this case," Jack remarked. "Of course, I'll have to come up with some sort of explanation for my fellow officers. They might not be quite so willing to believe in gifts like this."

"Maybe you could say I found a note that Mister Patterson left behind," Ken suggested.

"Mmm, that's not a bad idea. All right, Ken, you can go now. I'll have an officer take you back to school."

Paul was pleased. Now he'd be able to see what was going on in the gifted class, too. On the way to Meadowbrook, he pondered what he'd learned that day.

Ken was a hero, he thought. He used his gift, and he told the police where to find the bomb. Without Ken's help, the bomb might never have been found. It could have exploded and killed who knew how many people.

Amanda had been a hero, too. Paul had heard the story she told Dr. Paley in the office, about the hitchhiker. He'd heard everything else they talked about, too. Ken and Amanda . . . They had powerful gifts! Why did they want to lose them? He just didn't understand.

When they got back to Meadowbrook, Ken went to the administrative office to explain his absence. He was told to wait, and Paul worried that he wouldn't get to attend the gifted class after all.

"Amanda! What are you doing here?"

"I just wanted to see if you were back. What happened?"

There was another voice. "You may come in now, Ken. Amanda, what are you doing here?"

"Uh, just—uh, nothing."

"Then get right back to class." Then there was a gasp. "What's that?"

"What's what?" Amanda asked.

"I thought I saw a bug. It's gone now. Come in, Ken."

Back in Amanda's purse, Paul found a comfortable spot in an open packet of tissues. There wasn't much to listen to as Amanda went to her usual classes. She talked to her friends, but she didn't even mention the events of the morning. She couldn't, of course. Paul remembered how many times Madame told the class they shouldn't talk about their gifts to people who wouldn't understand. It gave him a thrill to think that this advice now applied to him, too.

But Amanda's conversations were so boring. He had to listen to her talk about some dumb TV show she had watched the night before, a sale at a shoe store, someone's new purse that was only a replica of a famous designer bag. And in the cafeteria, she made a huge fuss over chipping a fingernail. None of this made any sense to him at all.

He was getting hungry. He poked around through the contents of Amanda's purse and saw that most of the things weren't any more interesting than her conversations. He got a little case of lipgloss open with his nose. It smelled like raspberries, but when he licked the gooey pink stuff, it wasn't very tasty. A small bottle of perfume smelled nice, but he knew he wouldn't be able to get the top off, and the liquid inside would probably taste disgusting.

He lucked out when he found a granola bar. Working

on the paper for some time, he finally managed to make a tiny tear in the wrapper. Amanda wouldn't be too happy when she took out her bar and found it had been nibbled by a bug, but he couldn't help himself. After satisfying his hunger, he curled up in a silky scarf and went to sleep.

He woke up at the perfect time. Through the purse, he heard another familiar voice.

"Good afternoon, class. Where's Ken?"

He heard Amanda speak. "He's in the office, Madame. You won't believe what happened to us!"

Paul listened to Amanda tell the story of the man who committed suicide and the bomb he left behind.

"Oh my," Madame murmured. "How did Ken explain to the police why he knew where the bomb was?"

"I don't know," Amanda replied.

"And what were you and Ken doing there?"

Uh-oh, Paul thought. *She can't tell Madame they were consulting Doctor Paley.* He needed to help her out, provide a distraction. And he knew exactly how he could do it.

He crept out of her bag and started crawling up her leg. As he expected, Amanda let out an ear-piercing shriek and leaped out of her chair. Paul dropped to the floor and scurried away before Amanda could step on him.

"It's a cockroach! There are cockroaches in my purse!"

Somebody picked up a book and threw it at him. Paul dodged it and frantically searched the floorboards for a hole to crawl into. Then it dawned on him that here was the perfect opportunity to introduce his gift to the class. He shifted back to his human form.

"Carter!" Madame gasped. The rest of the class stared at him in stunned silence. The unfamiliar attention unnerved him, and it took a lot of effort to formulate any words. They came out as "I haff uh giff," but he was pretty sure they got the meaning.

Madame gazed at him in wonderment. "So I see," she said.

There was a short rap on the classroom door, and then the door opened. Dr. Paley walked in.

"Excuse me for interrupting your class, Madame," he said. "Ah, Paul. I thought I might find you here."

Madame's eyes darted back and forth between the boy and the doctor. "*Paul?*"

"That's his real name, the name he was given at birth," Dr. Paley said. "We're not sure about his last name, so we're calling him Paul Carter."

"Paul Carter," Madame repeated. "Well. We're pleased to have you back here, Paul."

"I'm afraid he can't stay," Dr. Paley said. "As you can see, Paul has made a lot of progress. He's recovered his memory, and he's beginning to speak."

"And he has a gift," Madame added.

"Yes, Paul is a shape shifter. But he still requires some counseling and therapy before he can be released from Harmony House. You'll have to come along with me, Paul."

Paul looked at Madame beseechingly, and Madame smiled but shook her head. "I'm sorry, Paul. We're all very excited about this, and we look forward to having you back, but you'll have to leave with Doctor Paley now."

Paul understood. As he walked to the door with the doctor, he looked at his classmates. Tracey and Emily smiled at him. Most of the others were looking at him in a friendly way, too. Only Jenna was frowning.

And Amanda, who had emptied the contents of her purse on her desk, was clearly upset. "He nibbled at my granola bar, Madame! That's gross!"

Chapter Sixteen

THE THOUGHT THAT A cockroach had been in her purse—even if that cockroach was really a human being—made Amanda sick. It wasn't just the granola bar. He could have crawled over everything. By the time she left class, she had decided to toss out everything that had been in her purse and replace it all with new stuff. First of all, she'd go directly to the mall and buy cosmetics. She'd need a new wallet, a replacement for her cell phone cover . . .

But all plans to restock her purse were swept away when she found Ken waiting for her by her locker.

"Ken, are you okay? What happened?"

Ken looked totally wiped out. He tried to smile, but it came out looking more like a grimace.

"I've been in the office all day, waiting to get a note for my absence." He sighed. "I had to tell him, Amanda."

"Tell who what?"

"Officer Fisher. I had to tell him about my gift."

Amanda drew in her breath. "No . . ."

"He kept asking me all these questions. And I couldn't come up with a story that would explain how I knew where the bomb was. I mean, what could I say? That I knew the guy who committed suicide and he told me what he was going to do? I didn't even know the poor man's name!" He leaned against the wall and let out a deep sigh. "So I told him I talk to dead people."

"What did he say?"

"He thought I was joking." Ken gave her a half-hearted smile. "You can't blame him. He told me I would have to come up with a better story than that. And I ended up telling him everything." He clenched his fists, and he looked like he was in real pain. "Everything, Amanda. Not just about me."

Now Amanda felt *really* sick. "You told him about our class? About all our gifts?"

"Well, I didn't go into details. But he knows we're a bunch of freaks." He sighed. "Madame is going to kill me."

"But he actually believed in your gift?" Amanda asked.

"Yeah, I guess so. Weird, huh? And then he let me go . . . but you should have seen the way he looked at me. Like I was some kind of alien." Suddenly he slammed his fist against the locker. "I hate this damned gift!"

Amanda had never seen him so upset. She touched his arm. "It's okay, Ken. It won't be for much longer. Tomorrow we'll see Doctor Paley and get that laser thing. No more gifts. We'll be normal."

"Shh," Ken whispered. Amanda turned to see Sarah coming toward them. She approached them tentatively, and when she spoke, her voice was barely audible.

"That was a very brave thing you did, Ken," she said.

He looked at her in confusion.

"I told the class how you located the bomb," Amanda explained.

"Oh." Ken forced a smile. "I wouldn't call it brave."

"Of course it was," Sarah said. "You revealed your gift so you could save people. I don't know if I would have the guts to do something like that."

"Maybe you'll never have to make the choice," Amanda said. "If you could lose your gift . . ." She looked at Ken with a question in her eyes. He shook his head slightly.

Sarah shrugged. "Well, I just wanted to say . . . I admire you."

"Thanks, Sarah," Ken said, and the girl left them.

"Why didn't you want me to tell her about Doctor Paley?" Amanda asked.

"I don't know," Ken said simply. "I guess, maybe because her gift is so powerful. And maybe she should hang on to it, because she could *really* save people."

"But if she doesn't *want* to save people," Amanda began and then clamped her mouth shut. Nina was there.

"Who's saving people?" she chirped.

Amanda had to press her lips together to keep herself from yelling "None of your business," but Ken actually smiled at Nina.

"The X-Men," he said. "We were just talking about what it would be like to have superpowers. What do you think?"

"Not a clue," Nina said blithely. "Anyone want to get an ice cream?"

Of course she was looking at Ken when she asked the question, but Amanda answered.

"No."

To her surprise—and extreme annoyance—Ken said, "Sounds good."

Amanda stared at them as they started toward the exit together. Then she hurried to catch up with them.

"I've changed my mind," she announced.

She didn't get it. Two minutes earlier, she and Ken had been having this intense, serious discussion. Now he was listening to Nina chatter about her day's activities—and actually paying attention.

". . . then Mister Jones called on me in history, and I hadn't read the assignment, so I started coughing and he let me go out to get some water, but when I got back, he asked me about the reading again, and so I started coughing again, and then . . ."

Ken seemed to be hanging on to every word. He kept his eyes on her, he nodded and made the right comments, like "no kidding" and "wow." Amanda couldn't believe it. Here she and Ken had just experienced this incredible day, and now he was acting like Nina was telling him something exciting.

How many more ways could she feel sick that day? she wondered as she slid into the booth at the ice-cream place. Was it possible that Ken was really into Nina? She couldn't bear this—she had to do something to turn him off her. And it dawned on her that she had the means to do this. She just had to come up with a reason to feel sorry for Nina . . .

". . . and if I don't get at least a C in history," Nina prattled, "I'll have to go to summer school, which means I won't be able to go to the beach . . ."

A summer without a tan. That was all it took.

CHAPTER SEVENTEEN

D R. PALEY WAS NOT happy with Paul. He didn't yell, and he didn't threaten to punish him, but on the way back to Harmony House, he gave Paul a lecture on what he should not do.

"You must not leave Harmony House without permission," he warned Paul. "You are not a prisoner there, but it is the one place where you are safe. Never forget that you are still in danger. The people who killed your parents are still out there, and they may still be looking for you. Do you understand?"

"Yes," Paul said, and he was pleased to hear the word come out correctly and clearly.

"And you must not shapeshift, except under controlled circumstances and in my presence. Your gift could put you in danger, too. If you became, say, a lion and went out into the street, people would become frightened.

You would be shot. Do you understand?"

"Yes," Paul said again. Why did Dr. Paley keep asking him if he understood? Paul wasn't stupid.

"Madame told me that you have always obeyed her orders," he continued. "You must obey my orders, too. Do you understand?"

"*Yes.*" The word came out louder this time. Dr. Paley took his eyes momentarily off the road to glance at him.

"Your voice is improving."

When they arrived back at Harmony House, Dr. Paley told him to go to his room. "I have an important meeting with my colleagues," he said. "I would like them to meet you. I'll send someone to get you when we're ready. And don't forget what I've told you."

Back in his room, Paul lay on his bed, stared at the ceiling, and thought about his little adventure. Visiting the gifted class had brought back all kinds of memories, mostly bad ones. He remembered himself sitting there day after day, not speaking, not thinking, responding to commands, following every order he was given, doing nothing on his own. He had been something not quite human.

Now he was human—and more. He could speak, he

could think. He had a gift. And he didn't have to follow orders anymore.

Like the orders Dr. Paley gave him just now. He knew the doctor was trying to protect him, and there was a time when Paul only wanted to be protected. That was why he followed orders, because he was always afraid.

He wasn't afraid anymore. And he didn't want to stay in this room and wait for Dr. Paley to send for him. There was so much to see, so much to explore. And hear. He was curious about Dr. Paley's meeting with his colleagues—people who believed in unusual gifts and what could be done with them. He could learn more about himself. Clearly, Dr. Paley thought he wasn't terribly intelligent, or he wouldn't be constantly asking Paul if he understood. So he wasn't going to get a lot of information from him, not right away at least. He wanted to hear Dr. Paley and his colleagues speaking freely.

He considered his options. What could he become? He didn't particularly want to be a cockroach again. True, he had to be small so no one would notice him, but he wanted to try something new. A spider? No, he could easily be stepped on and crushed. A snake? No. A worm . . . but they couldn't move very fast. His plan was to go to Dr. Paley's office, listen to their conversation, and then, as soon as the doctor sent for him, return to his room and shift back.

He was going to have to be a mouse, he decided. There were mice all over this building—the doctor had said so himself. And they weren't all shapeshifting humans. If by any chance he was spotted, no one would be too shocked.

Maybe a white mouse, not the ordinary gray kind. White ones were nicer looking. After he shifted, he wished he could get up to the mirror over the sink so he could admire himself, but it was just too high.

He slipped out under the door and looked around. No one was in the hall, but even so, he kept close to the wall. As he approached Dr. Paley's office, he heard voices coming from around the corner, so he dived under the door of the office next to the doctor's.

Big mistake. "Eek, a mouse!" someone screamed. So people were just as freaked out by white mice as they were by gray ones. Paul raced along the edge of the room until he came to a hole just big enough to squeeze through. He spotted another mouse in the cavity, but he didn't pay any attention to Paul. That was good—

Paul had no idea how mice communicated with each other.

He could hear people chattering excitedly through the wall of the room he'd just left.

"Those traps we set are not working," one person said. "We have to call in some real exterminators."

Paul shuddered. Well, he didn't have to stay being a mouse forever. But he would have to keep an eye out for those traps. What was it people put in traps to attract mice? Cheese, right? Paul wasn't too worried. He didn't like cheese. It would be no temptation for him.

He followed a narrow tunnel in what he thought was the direction of Dr. Paley's office. Sure enough, after a moment, he was able to make out some other voices, including one that he recognized.

"It's a phenomenal situation," the doctor was saying. "Nine students, and each one has a different gift."

"Which ones are coming for the procedure tomorrow?" another voice asked.

"The bodysnatching girl and the boy who talks to the deceased."

"What about the controller? She's the most intriguing."

"Supposedly, according to the subjects I spoke with, she wants to lose her gift, too, and I encouraged them to bring her along."

Then a third voice, a woman this time. "Is it really necessary to perform the procedure? We could learn so much from these kids. And think of their potential for investigation, advances in medicine and psychology, diplomacy . . . These kids could end wars!"

"Or start them," Dr. Paley said. "They're too young and immature—they can't be trusted with these powers."

"But we could work with them," the woman said. "Keep them in a controlled environment, train them, so they'd want to use their gifts for positive purposes."

"That's what the teacher is trying to do," Dr. Paley said. "But it's impossible. The subjects are too strong; they can't be contained. Already the subjects have fallen into the wrong hands on several occasions. They're dangerous."

"The potential is frightening," the other male voice concurred. "We really have no option. Their gifts must be eliminated."

"And we need to begin immediately," Dr. Paley said.

He must have moved farther from the wall because his voice became fainter, but Paul could still hear him.

"Ms. Callow? Would you send a resident assistant to bring Paul Carter here?"

This was Paul's cue. He needed to take off, get back to his room, and shift before the resident assistant appeared.

But he didn't move. He had to hear more. And it was a good thing he did.

"I'm looking forward to observing the procedures tomorrow," the male voice said.

"Actually, I don't think that's a good idea," Dr. Paley told him. "I haven't requested approval for the procedure from the Harmony House administrators."

"Why not?"

"Because it's quite possible they would have refused. It's still a highly experimental surgery. My appointments with the two students are on the books, and it might look peculiar if I have all of you here, too."

"That's a shame," the other man said. "I wanted to

see if there would be immediate results. And any possible side effects."

"You will," Dr. Paley said. "That's what we're going to find out right now. I'll do the procedure on Paul."

"Does he want to lose his gift?" the woman asked.

"He doesn't know what he wants," Dr. Paley replied. "I don't think he has any sense of what his gift really entails. Don't worry, he won't give us any problems. If he shifts, I'll have a tranquilizer gun ready to knock him out, whatever he becomes."

"But what about the others?" the woman asked. "You said that two of the students are coming for the procedure voluntarily tomorrow, but what about the other six students?"

"What about them?" Dr. Paley countered.

"Maybe they don't want to lose their gifts," the woman said. "What if they refuse to have the procedure?"

There was a moment of silence before Dr. Paley replied. His tone was grim.

"Then the subjects themselves must be eliminated."

CHAPTER EIGHTEEN

"NINA?"

Amanda-Nina blinked rapidly. It always took her a minute or so to adjust to being in another body. "What?"

"Are you okay?" Ken asked.

"Sure. Anyway, let's see, what were we talking about?" She did what she hoped sounded like a typical Nina giggle. "I'm such a ditz sometimes!"

"About how you might have to go to summer school."

Could he really be interested in this? Amanda wondered. "Yeah, isn't that lame? What am I going to do? Maybe I can bribe someone to write the next essay for me. And there's this really nerdy girl in the class. I bet she'd let me cheat off her if I let her sit with my group at lunch one time."

She watched Ken carefully as she spoke. He was pretty

much the honorable type—he'd rather fail an exam than cheat to pass it. And he'd never approved of the snobbishness of some cliques and the way the girls acted like they were superior to other people. This had to be turning him off Nina.

He got up. "I'm going to the bathroom. If the waitress comes, could you order me a chocolate milkshake?"

"Okey-dokey!" Amanda-Nina said brightly.

She took advantage of Ken's absence to check on her *own* body. Other-Amanda had taken out her makeup bag, and she was filing her nails. Why was she always doing that? Amanda wondered. Real Amanda didn't file her nails *that* much. And what if that disgusting bug had crawled over the file? Amanda-Nina shuddered.

It occurred to her that she'd never spoken to her robotself before. She tried now.

"A cockroach was on that nail file," she informed her.

"Ick!" Other-Amanda exclaimed, and she dropped the file.

Not bad, Amanda-Nina thought. That was pretty much what she would have done in the same circumstances. And now what would the robot do?

Exactly what real Amanda would have done. "I have to wash my hands!" she cried out. She left the booth and practically ran toward the bathroom. Amanda watched with interest. She'd never had such a good view of that dress from the back. Maybe she'd ask her mother to hem it, make it a little shorter.

A waitress came to the booth. "Hi. What can I get for you?"

"My friend wants a chocolate milkshake. I'll have . . ." She was about to ask for a diet soda but thought better of it. "A hot fudge sundae." After all, she'd be packing the calories on Nina's body, not her own.

"And the other person?"

"Water." It wasn't like Other-Amanda could really taste anything. And she began to wonder if maybe she should continue occupying Nina through the next day. Dr. Paley had said the procedure wouldn't hurt, but Amanda wouldn't mind letting the robot endure it instead of her. But no, the last time Ken had been with Other-Amanda, the thing had completely turned him off. Besides, this was something they had to do together.

Which brought her back to the immediate situation.

She had to hold on to Ken's attention now so he wouldn't realize that the person he thought was Amanda had become the robot. This would not be easy, to keep his attention and turn him off simultaneously.

He was returning to the table now, followed closely behind by Other-Amanda. They both got into the booth.

"Nina, I was thinking," Ken said. "I've got Jones for history, too, and I'm doing pretty well in his class. Maybe I could help you. We could study together."

Amanda-Nina tried very hard not to let Nina's face show what she, Amanda, was feeling. It was worse than she thought. Ken wanted to get close to Nina! This made no sense at all to her. Nina was everything Ken didn't like—snotty, shallow, and selfish. She forced herself to giggle.

"Study? Ick! Who has time to study? I'd rather go to the mall after school."

"In the evenings," Ken suggested.

The waitress appeared with their orders. She put the glass of water down in front of Other-Amanda, who reached into her purse, pulled out her iPod, and stuck the earphones into her ears. Then she dropped a straw into the glass and started to sip. Amanda-Nina wouldn't have to worry about her.

Ken barely glanced at his milkshake. The hot fudge sundae in front of Amanda-Nina looked delicious, but she couldn't waste time on it.

"In the evenings? And miss all my favorite TV shows?" She started counting them off on her fingers. "*America's Next Top Model. Real World. American Idol. The Real Housewives of New Jersey.*"

Finally, a glimmer of distaste crossed Ken's face. "You like those reality shows?"

"*Love* them! Don't you?"

"Well . . . I guess I've never actually seen any of them," Ken said. "Maybe we can watch them together."

Amanda-Nina stared at him in disbelief. Ken hated reality TV—he'd told her that before. He thought these shows were stupid, and he couldn't understand why so many of his classmates liked them.

And that was when it hit her. Their classmates . . . Their ordinary, normal classmates who did ordinary, normal things, like go to the mall and watch TV. Who didn't go around snatching other people's bodies or talking to dead people. Nina was one of those ordinary, normal people, and Ken wanted to be one, too. That was why he wanted to connect with Nina.

An enormous wave of sadness came over her. Nina might be ordinary, but Ken deserved so much better. He deserved her, Amanda. Not the robot, who was now sitting placidly in her seat, sipping her water and listening to her iPod. Real Amanda. She amended that. Real un-gifted Amanda. And if he could just hold on till they had their procedures, they'd both be normal and they could be normal *together*.

She was desperate. "Do you really want to hang out with me, Ken? I'm not that smart, you know. I don't read at all. I'm not interested in current events. All I ever want to do is shop, and . . . and style my hair, and stuff like that. I don't really think we're right for each other."

Ken looked confused, and Amanda-Nina couldn't blame him. Nina had been coming on to him for days now, and here she was telling him she wasn't interested in hanging out together! She couldn't go on like this. Quickly, she gobbled three big spoonfuls of the sundae. Then she focused on the robot.

Easy-peasy. Amanda pulled out the earphones.

"Nina, are you feeling all right?"

A dazed-looking Nina stared at the hot fudge sundae in front of her. "Where did that come from?" She rubbed her head. "Did I faint or something?"

"You're not well," Amanda said firmly. "Come on, I'll walk you home." She gave Nina a little push, and Nina got herself out of the booth.

Ken's eyes darted back and forth between the two girls and settled on Amanda. Then suddenly he grinned. "That was you," he said.

"What's he talking about?" Nina asked.

"Nothing," Amanda said. She heard a little dinging sound that told her she had a text message on her cell phone. A second later, a ding came from Ken's, too.

Taking the phone out of her purse, Amanda looked for the message.

Please be in my office at 10:00 Friday morning.

She was pretty sure that Ken was reading the very same message on his phone. They looked at each other.

"Tomorrow?" Amanda asked.

He nodded. "Tomorrow."

Chapter Nineteen

PAUL CARTER, THE WHITE mouse, had been through a rough night. When Dr. Paley learned that Paul wasn't in his room, he'd become anxious. He'd had the institution locked down—no one could go in or out—and all the staff were alerted to be on the lookout for him. Paul didn't dare leave the wall cavity, not even as a mouse.

So Dr. Paley planned to take all the gifts away from the students. And if all the gifted students didn't voluntarily submit to his "procedure," the students would be eliminated. He didn't hear Dr. Paley explain how this would be done, but Paul didn't doubt that he would find a way. And Madame trusted this man. She wouldn't guess his intentions, and she would probably give him access to Paul's classmates.

In a strange way, Paul understood the doctor's plans. And he didn't even think the doctor was evil—not like

Serena Hancock, or the kidnapper Clare, or Mr. Jackson, the former principal. Dr. Paley truly believed that the gifted students were dangerous, that they presented a threat to the world. And he believed he was doing what was best for society.

Only it wasn't the best for Paul, or Amanda, or Ken, or any of his classmates. Dr. Paley had to be stopped. And Paul was the only one who knew or cared about what Dr. Paley wanted to do. He would have to stop him.

But Paul was a mouse, a tiny, insignificant creature that couldn't do much worse than chew through a granola bar wrapper a little more efficiently than a cockroach could.

Throughout the night, he wandered the narrow tunnels and crevices in the walls. It was cold in there, and he was hungry. But for the first time in a very long time, cold and hunger didn't matter so much to him. He had more important things to think about.

He did have one other option. If mice had gotten into the building, there had to be a way out. If he could find an exit and get far enough away so no one from Harmony House could see him, he could shift back into himself.

He could seek out Amanda or Ken or Madame and warn them. But even though he'd lost track of the time in his wanderings, he knew it had to be the middle of the night. His classmates, his teacher—none of them would be at school. He had no idea where any of them lived, or even how to contact them by phone—and even if he did manage to contact them, how could he make himself understood?

But at least you'd be able to escape Doctor Paley yourself, he thought. He could go anywhere. He could live in a zoo for a while. Become a bird and fly to a distant land. Or become a squirrel and live in a tree, feeding on berries and nuts. Nobody bothered squirrels.

Only he didn't want to run away. He wanted to stay who he was—well, not who he was at that very moment. He wanted to be a boy. He wanted to go back to his foster family. He'd never been able to talk to the Grangers, to have any real contact with them, but he knew they'd been kind to him. He wanted to find out what kind of people they were and why they took in foster children. He wanted to get to know the two other boys he'd been living with. Maybe they'd play games together. Maybe they could have fun.

And more than anything, he wanted to be back at Meadowbrook Middle School, in room 209. He wanted to know the other special gifted students, to become part of their world—to learn how they could all use their gifts to make the world a better place, so that the kind of people who killed his parents couldn't get away with their crimes. What was it Madame had told them they could do? Benefit mankind. They could do that together. Running away, he'd just be alone again. A thing.

No, he had to stay and find some way to stop Dr. Paley and his colleagues. So he made his way through the walls and back to the place where he knew he was just outside the office. And he waited.

He slept a little, off and on, but the hunger and the cold didn't let him stay asleep very long. When some light came through a crack in the wall, he knew that it must be morning. And soon after that, he heard voices.

"Ms. Callow, I've got two young people coming at ten, and I don't want to be disturbed while they're in the office with me. Not even if it's important."

"Yes, sir. Oh, and sir?"

"Yes, Ms. Callow?"

"The Carter boy still hasn't been located."

Dr. Paley let out a deep sigh. "Well . . . if a strange animal appears in the building . . . a lion, or a tiger, whatever it is . . . tell security not to shoot it. They can tranquilize the animal, but they shouldn't try to kill it."

There was a moment before the secretary choked out, "Sir?"

Dr. Paley must have been a quick thinker. "I just heard on the radio about some animals escaping from the zoo. That's all."

"I see. Yes, sir. I'll notify security."

He really doesn't want to kill us, Paul thought. *That's a last resort. It's because he's afraid of us.* He himself had spent such a long time being afraid. It was a strange sensation, thinking someone might be afraid of *him*.

He examined the wall, feeling his way along as he searched for a hole big enough to let him get into the office. He was in luck—another mouse came from the opposite direction. Obviously, that little guy knew the area well. He disappeared from the tunnel. A second later, he heard Dr. Paley curse.

"Ms. Callow, please send another memo to the

director. Something has to be done about these mice."

"Yes, sir."

Paul made his way to the point where the other mouse had escaped from the tunnel. All thoughts of hunger and cold and fatigue had vanished. He perched on his hind legs and peered out.

He could see Dr. Paley's feet. The man was walking around the office. Paul could hear things being picked up, put down, moved around. *The doctor must be setting things up for the procedure*, Paul thought.

He settled down to wait.

Chapter Twenty

"HE SAID IT WOULDN'T hurt, right?" Amanda asked Ken as they approached Harmony House. "Do you believe him? I remember when I was a little kid, that's what doctors always said before they gave you an injection. And it hurt."

Ken nodded. "I know. But my mother had laser surgery on her eyes to improve her vision. She said she couldn't feel a thing."

"Okay." She felt Ken take her hand, and a tingle went up her arm.

"It's going to be fine," he said. "We're doing the right thing. I think."

"Absolutely," Amanda affirmed. "This is what we want. To be normal."

"I mean, it's not like I'll be looking for hidden bombs set by dead people again," Ken went on. "And you're not going to run into hitchhikers every day."

"Of course not," Amanda assured him. "And remember that boy who was looking for the lottery ticket his father had put away before he died? I bet he would have found it eventually, even without your help."

"Maybe," Ken said. "Probably." After a moment, he added, "No, you're absolutely, positively right. He would have found it."

They entered the building and went up to the receptionist. "We have an appointment with Doctor Paley," Amanda said and gave her their names.

The woman checked her computer screen. "Yes, you can proceed to his office."

Her actions and response put Amanda at ease. This was just like going to the dentist, she thought. Easier, in fact. No injections, no drilling. This was more like going to the hair salon. It was no big deal.

And the secretary in the doctor's outer office was equally reassuring.

"Doctor Paley is expecting you," she said with a nod. "Go right in."

The doctor greeted them with a warm and welcoming smile. "Hello, Ken, Amanda. How are you feeling?"

"A little nervous," Ken admitted.

"But we haven't changed our minds," Amanda added quickly.

"Good," Dr. Paley said. "As I told you before, it's experimental surgery, but tests have indicated no side effects or problems associated with the procedure. You won't feel a thing. And since there's no an anaesthetic, you won't need any recovery time."

"When my mother had laser surgery on her eyes, she did it during her lunch break and went right back to work afterward," Ken said.

Dr. Paley nodded. "And you'll be able to go right back to school." Then he grinned. "Unless you want an excuse to cut classes. I'll even write you a note. There's always a very slight possibility you'll experience a mild headache later today, but nothing that can't be cured with a regular pain reliever."

Amanda turned to Ken. "We could buy some sandwiches and have a picnic lunch in the park."

"Okay," Ken said. Amanda thought he looked a little pale. He was still holding her hand, and she gave it a squeeze.

Dr. Paley moved a machine toward them. "First I need

to take scans of your heads. You've both had scans before, haven't you? You know it's nothing to be afraid of."

That procedure took all of two minutes. Afterward, Dr. Paley studied the images of their heads on a lighted screen.

"Yes," he murmured, more to himself than to them. "This won't be difficult at all." He addressed them. "I'd like to run a little test first, just to make sure I've pinpointed the area accurately." He studied them both for a moment. "Amanda . . . you have more control over your gift than Ken does, don't you?"

Amanda hesitated. She didn't want to hurt Ken's feelings. She knew that some boys could get totally unnerved if they learned a girl could do something better than they could. Fortunately, Ken wasn't that kind of boy.

"Totally," Ken said. "It's hard to call a dead person. I usually have to wait for someone to contact me first. Amanda can pretty much snap her fingers and become another person."

Amanda lowered her eyes modestly. "Oh, it's not *that* easy, Ken. I mean, I have to concentrate. And I need to find something depressing about the person."

186

Ken grinned. "That wasn't too hard with Nina, was it? It must be pretty easy to feel sorry for someone that boring."

Amanda giggled.

Dr. Paley looked like he was getting impatient. "All right, then let's get on with the little test. Amanda, you need to feel pity for your subject. Did you notice my secretary, Ms. Callow?"

Amanda hadn't really paid any attention to the woman in the outer office. "What about her?"

"Ms. Callow has a sad life," the doctor told her. "She was very much in love with a man, and they were about to get married when he was killed in an accident. In fact, this happened on the way to the wedding ceremony."

"How awful!" Amanda exclaimed.

"Now she lives in a tiny apartment with her elderly mother, who's always nagging her."

"Why doesn't she just move out?" Amanda wanted to know.

"Her mother is not well and requires a great deal of care."

"Can't she hire someone to do it?"

Dr. Paley shook his head. "Ms. Callow cannot afford a nurse, so she has to do everything herself. She takes care of her mother in the morning, works here all day, then goes home to take care of her mother in the evenings. She has no social life at all. She's never even had a vacation, since her mother can't travel and Ms. Callow can't leave her alone."

Amanda frowned. She thought doctors were rich. "Couldn't you give her some money so she could hire someone to stay with her mother?"

Dr. Paley seemed momentarily annoyed by the question, but he recovered quickly. "I've offered, of course. But she's very proud. She won't accept charity. So she suffers."

It all sounded pretty grim to Amanda. That poor woman—what a depressing life she led.

Dr. Paley watched her expression closely. Then he went to the door and opened it. "Ms. Callow, could you come in here for a minute?"

For the first time, Amanda gave the secretary a long, hard look. She was attractive, and her clothes were decent. Cute, even. The woman didn't seem all that miserable. But appearances were deceptive—she knew that. Ms. Callow probably put up a good front for her job. Maybe she wore that same suit every day. This image made Amanda feel even more sympathy for her.

Dr. Paley spoke quietly to the secretary. "Please remain very still and don't say anything. I'm running a test." He went to his table of instruments and picked up a thick tube with a rubbery tip. Amanda flinched as he approached her with it.

"This won't hurt," he assured her. "I'm only going to touch your scalp with it."

He was telling the truth. It didn't hurt at all—there was just a little pressure.

"Now, Amanda, take over Ms. Callow."

"What?" the secretary cried out in alarm.

"Be quiet," the doctor ordered. "Go ahead, Amanda."

Amanda looked at the secretary and tried to imagine her daily life. All alone, except for her old mother, who probably wasn't very good company if she was sick all the time. She pictured a dark, ugly apartment and empty closets. Pity overwhelmed her.

"Amanda?"

Amanda looked at the doctor in wonderment. "I'm still me!"

Dr. Paley removed the instrument. "Excellent. You may leave, Ms. Callow."

The confused-looking secretary retreated and closed the door behind her.

"I have accurately pinpointed the area we need to treat," the doctor said. "Ken, I wish I could test you, but . . . Ken? Are you listening to me?"

Amanda looked at Ken. She recognized the glazed expression on her classmate's face.

"He's hearing someone! Ken, is it the soap opera lady?"

Dr. Paley didn't wait for Ken's response. He hurried over to him and pressed the rubber thing against his skull.

Ken frowned. "Jack . . . ?" He blinked.

"That's his friend—the one who died after the collision," Amanda told Dr. Paley.

"Jack?" Ken murmured again.

Dr. Paley smiled in satisfaction and lifted the instrument. "I cut the connection, Ken. This is going to work very well. I have no doubts." He nodded toward the examining table. "Who wants to go first?"

Ken and Amanda looked at each other. "Ladies first?" Ken suggested.

"Oh, that's so old-fashioned," Amanda said quickly.

Dr. Paley smiled. "Okay, I'll decide. Come on, Ken, let's show the young lady there's nothing to be afraid of."

Ken climbed up on to the table and lay down.

"I'll use the scan to pinpoint the exact spot where I'll direct the laser beam," the doctor said. He wheeled the machine to the side of the table.

Amanda watched nervously, but a movement on the floor distracted her. "There's a mouse!" she cried out.

Ken sat up. "Where?"

Amanda couldn't answer him. She couldn't even speak. Before her eyes, the mouse began to expand, and its body changed form. Then it wasn't a mouse at all.

"Carter!" she exclaimed.

"His name's Paul," Ken reminded her.

"Whatever," Amanda replied. "What are you doing here?"

Dr. Paley was frowning. "Paul, you shouldn't be in here. Go to your room immediately."

The boy's mouth moved, as if he was trying to reply. The only word that came out was "No."

Amanda glared at the boy. "I can't believe you nibbled at my granola bar. That was so disgusting."

Dr. Paley went to the door and opened it. "Ms. Callow, would you please call a resident assistant to escort Paul Carter back to his room?

The secretary came to the door and stared at Paul in astonishment. "I didn't even see him come in!"

"Um, he was hiding in the cabinet," Dr. Paley told her. "It's not important. Just call for a resident assistant, please." Ms. Callow hurriedly went back out to her desk.

Paul looked at Ken. Amanda remembered how expressionless the boy usually looked. Now there was no mistaking the urgency on his face.

"Stop," Paul said.

"Stop what?" Ken asked.

He mumbled something that sounded like "dun loose ya giff."

"We can't understand a word you're saying," Amanda snapped impatiently.

A familiar voice came from outside the door. "He's

saying, don't lose your gift."

"You can't go in there!" Ms. Callow yelled.

But as usual, Jenna didn't respond well to authority figures. She stomped right into Dr. Paley's office.

"What are *you* doing here?" Ken asked.

"If you want the procedure, you're going to have to wait your turn," Amanda snapped.

Jenna wasn't alone. The police officer, Jack Fisher, followed her into Dr. Paley's office.

The doctor was not pleased. "Excuse me, but we're in the process of a medical procedure here!"

"No one's performing any procedures in here today," Officer Fisher declared. "This surgery has not been authorized by Harmony House officials."

"What are you talking about?" Dr. Paley sputtered. "I am a certified medical doctor. I don't have to ask permission to perform a simple procedure that doesn't require an anaesthetic."

"You do when it's an experimental operation," the policeman declared.

"And what makes you think I'm doing an experimental operation?" the doctor demanded to know.

"This young lady told me."

Dr. Paley stared at Jenna. Jenna stared right back at him.

"You weren't very careful, Doctor Paley," she said. "You know about my gift. You know what I'm able to do. But you didn't block me when you came into class yesterday. I read your mind."

Dr. Paley turned to the police officer. "And you believe this nonsense? Do you honestly think this girl can read minds?"

"Yes," Jack Fisher said simply. "Just as I believe that boy on the table can communicate with the dead."

And then another person came into the room. "Doctor Paley, please don't bother my students," Madame said quietly.

The doctor dropped all pretense. "Madame, I have no choice. This is absolutely necessary."

"Why?" she demanded to know.

"Because your students are dangerous."

Madame corrected him. "My students have the *potential* to be dangerous, just as all people have. But my students also have the potential to do great and wondrous things. I will not allow you to take that potential away from them."

Amanda finally got a chance to get a word in. "But Madame," she wailed, "I don't want to do great and wondrous things. I want to be normal! And so does Ken!"

"Do you, Ken?" Jack asked. "Yesterday you saved lives. Maybe hundreds of them. Could a normal person do that?"

Amanda looked at Ken. He seemed torn. He clenched his fists, his eyebrows went up, and he mumbled, "Not now, Jack."

"Excuse me?" the police officer said.

"Not you, sir. I'm talking to my friend Jack. I'll get back to you later, buddy." Then he hopped off the table.

"Amanda, maybe they're right. Maybe we shouldn't give this up. Think about the hitchhiker you saved."

"But think about me!" Amanda protested. "I don't want to spend my life hopping in and out of other people!"

"Oh, come on, Amanda," Ken said. "You've got more control over your gift than half the people in our class. You can choose when to use it."

Amanda had to admit he had a point.

"And what's so great about being normal, anyway?" Ken continued. "Think of your friend Nina. You want to be like her?"

Another good point. And what he said cheered her. Clearly, he wasn't impressed with her frenemy.

"I wish I could arrest you," Jack said to the doctor. "I wish I could take you into custody right now. Unfortunately, I can't prove that you're doing anything illegal. But I'll be keeping my eyes on you from now on, Doctor."

"I'm taking my students back to school now," Madame told Dr. Paley. "Including Paul."

"He hasn't been released from Harmony House," Dr. Paley argued.

"That can be arranged," Jack Fisher said. "I do have some influence here, you know. And I'm going to get a court order to keep you away from the gifted students."

The doctor turned to Madame. "You're going to regret this. When these young people get a little older, when they begin making their own calculated decisions how and when and why to use these gifts, you'll find that you've enabled and released unimaginable horror."

Amanda expected Madame to defend them. But instead, the teacher sighed. "Perhaps. I don't blame you for being frightened. I've got students who are afraid of their own gifts."

"As well they should be," Dr. Paley declared.

Madame nodded. "I can only hope to influence them, to help them use their gifts wisely and well. Some of them may reject this, but it's a risk I'm willing to take."

Amanda's eyes went from Ken to Jenna to Paul and she shivered. Who knew what any of them could turn out to be? Good, bad—there was no way of knowing. But there was one thing she knew for sure: their lives wouldn't be boring.

"Come along, class," Madame said. And Dr. Paley stepped aside to allow the gifted students to leave.

CHAPTER TWENTY-ONE

ON MONDAY MORNING, PAUL Carter took his place in the gifted class, just behind Martin.

Martin turned around. "What did it feel like, being a cockroach?"

Paul tried to answer. "Like . . . a cockroach." The last word came out sounding more like "rush," but Martin got the idea.

"Gross," he said.

Paul nodded. He thought about Martin's gift, and wondered if he'd ever be able to use his strength whenever he wanted to. What would he use it to do?

He looked around the room at his other classmates. Charles . . . Someday he wouldn't be satisfied with using his gift just to make his life easier. Maybe he would stop a bullet from reaching its target and save a life. Or maybe he'd send two cars crashing into each other, just to amuse himself.

Emily . . . Could she rescue an entire city by warning the inhabitants of an impending earthquake? Or would she refuse to focus her gift and just allow fragments of visions to pass through her head?

Jenna could know good intentions and evil intentions, and she could take action—or refuse to get involved. Tracey could be a spy, but for what purposes? Ken could channel the dead and learn from them to help the living . . . or maybe he'd just watch soap operas. Amanda could make someone's life better. She could also make it worse.

His eyes rested on Sarah. He felt like he understood her now and why she was so afraid. In a way, she was like Dr. Paley. She recognized the terrible possibilities of her gift. She didn't trust herself to be able to use it well. The temptations might be too great.

Paul could relate to that. So far, it had come easy for him. His gift had been used to hide and to escape. It grew out of fear. He'd learned over the past few days that it could be used to inspire fear. Not just Amanda's fear of cockroaches and mice—much greater fears than that.

So perhaps Dr. Paley was right to want them un-gifted, or even eliminated. Or maybe Madame was right in believing they could benefit mankind.

He hoped Madame would talk about this today. About all the dangers they faced—from people like Serena, Mr. Jackson, Clare, the people who wanted to use their gifts for some terrible purpose. People like Dr. Paley, who wanted to take their gifts away. And people like themselves.

He had a lot to learn—about himself, about his classmates, about what they could do, individually and together. And as Madame entered the room and called the class to order, he sat back and began to listen.

Nine powers that can change the world.

Other titles available:

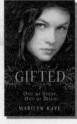

1. OUT OF SIGHT, OUT OF MIND
One morning Amanda looked in the
mirror and another girl looked back.

2. BETTER LATE THAN NEVER
Jenna can read anyone's mind, but her
long-lost dad is a total mystery.

3. HERE TODAY, GONE TOMORROW
Emily can see into the future, but her
visions show nothing but trouble.

4. FINDERS KEEPERS
Ken is a popular guy—
especially with dead people.

5. NOW YOU SEE ME
Tracey can make herself invisible—a gift
that comes with definite advantages.

www.giftedseries.com